CHECKPOINTS

CHECKPOINTS

Marilyn Levy

2008 • 5768
Philadelphia

JPS is a nonprofit educational association and the oldest and foremost publisher of Judaica in English in North America. The mission of JPS is to enhance Jewish culture by promoting the dissemination of religious and secular works, in the United States and abroad, to all individuals and institutions interested in past and contemporary Jewish life.

The Jewish Publication Society
2100 Arch Street, 2nd floor
Philadelphia, PA 19103
www.jewishpub.org

Cover illustration and design by Avi Katz
Design and Composition by Claudia Cappelli

Manufactured in the United States of America

Library of Congress Cataloging-in-Publication Data

Levy, Marilyn.
  Checkpoints / Marilyn Levy. -- 1st ed.
      p. cm.
Summary: Tensions in 2002 Jerusalem have not interfered much with sixteen-year-old Noa's life, and she is even forming a friendship with a Palestinian Muslim girl, but the Passover suicide bombing in Netanya changes Noa's family forever and transforms her faith, politics, and friendships.

      ISBN 978-0-8276-0870-2 (alk. paper)

      1. Arab-Israeli conflict—1993—Juvenile fiction. [1. Arab-Israeli conflict—1993—Fiction. 2. Race relations—Fiction. 3. Family life—Jerusalem—Fiction. 4. Suicide bombings—Fiction. 5. Terrorism—Fiction. 6. Jews--Israel—Fiction. 7. Netanyah (Israel)—Fiction. 8. Israel—Fiction.] I. Title.
      PZ7.L58325Che 2008
      [Fic]—dc22
                                          2008011437

JPS books are available at discounts for bulk purchases for reading groups, special sales, and fundraising purchases. Custom editions, including personalized covers, can be created in larger quantities for special needs. For more information, please contact us at marketing@jewishpub.org or at this address: 2100 Arch Street, Philadelphia, PA 19103.

For those who seek to build bridges

Although the Passover suicide bombing at the Park Hotel in Netanya was an actual event, all situations and characters in this book are purely a creation of the author's imagination and have no relation to any of the victims of that tragedy or their families.

ACKNOWLEDGMENTS

My appreciation and thanks to my editor, Rena Potok, for her invaluable suggestions and for pushing me to keep revising the manuscript; to Janet L. Liss, managing editor, who responded to all of my annoying questions; to my copyeditor Christine Sweeney, who did a heroic job that went beyond the call of duty; to Daniella Deutsch, who pointed me in the right direction; to Lawrence Levy for his insight and support; to Meira Aboulafia for serving as my personal reference library; and to Monica Koplow for her copious suggestions.

CHAPTER

1

There are things I can't explain, feelings that go deeper than words. Still, I'll try to tell you my story, though it's not just my story. My story is part of a much bigger story, one that includes my family, my country, and an endless war that isn't called a war.

It's hard to know where to start. It seems as if we've always lived this way. I've never known what it's like to go into a department store or movie theater where there isn't a guard at the entrance checking purses and backpacks. It's just the way things are, and in a sense the situation didn't really affect me. I had friends, listened to music, and went to parties, studied—well, maybe not always as hard as I could have.

But I guess I began seeing things differently that Thursday night in February 2002 when I visited my sister at the university. The evening began like lots of other evenings. We were just a group of kids out for a good time.

Eight of us sat crowded around a tiny table at the Moment Café. We were laughing, arguing, talking loudly, ignoring the rock music blaring in the background. Some of us were even flirting a little. I was trying to act cool and not doing a very good job of it.

"So, Noa, how come Shoshanna's never brought you around before?" Rafi asked. And he winked at me.

I was embarrassed and thrilled at the same time. "Maybe she's afraid of the competition," I shot back.

Everyone laughed, including my sister, Shoshanna. Rafi gave me a high five.

"Watch it, Rafi, Noa's only sixteen," Tamar said.

"You guys aren't that much older," I insisted, as I tossed back my hair the way my sister does.

"I'm only looking," Rafi protested.

"When'd you get back?" Gideon asked Shoshanna. "I phoned you last night to set up a rehearsal time."

"This morning. I didn't have a chance to call you."

"How'd the concert go?" someone wanted to know.

1

"It was okay," Shoshanna said. But we all knew it had probably been more than okay.

Shoshanna started playing the violin when she turned four. She was a prodigy. She tried to live as normal a life as possible; going to college, having friends, eating pizza, but she spent at least three hours a day practicing. Usually more. No matter what, her music came first—before friends, before family, before her classes at the university. To be honest, I used to resent it sometimes. When she was practicing, my brother, Ari, and I had to be quiet. This was harder on me than on Ari. For one thing, he's three years older than I am, and he could go off with his friends. For another thing, even though I'm a girl, I tend to be much noisier than Ari, or anyone else in the family, for that matter.

"So how was it in Germany?" Rafi asked.

"They're concerned about what's going on here, if that's what you mean," Shoshanna answered.

"It's kind of scary everywhere right now."

"No kidding."

"Not like here, though."

"Not yet, maybe."

Everyone at our table was quiet for a moment. I glanced at Gideon and saw that he was really into the music, so I felt free to stare at him. Gideon is a cellist and has a musician's ability to focus totally on each note, blocking out everything else. He's twenty-one, a year older than Shoshanna. Very dark and handsome, sort of mysterious. He seemed to live a very interesting and complicated life. I tried to wrangle a place next to him that night, but Tamar slipped in beside him before I could grab the seat.

Gideon likes girls, in general, I think. I know he liked Shoshanna even then, but she wasn't all that interested in him. She said he was too flaky for her. Me? I didn't care if he was flaky.

When Shoshanna said she was tired, we got up to leave. I was disappointed; I really wanted to stay longer.

"Noa doesn't have school tomorrow, so she's staying in the dorm with me tonight and tomorrow night. We can rehearse after she leaves on Saturday," she told Gideon. But I jumped right in and said, "Hey, I'd love to listen to you guys practice."

Shoshanna looked at me for a moment. I think she was trying to decide if I could keep quiet for more than ten minutes while she and Gideon were rehearsing.

Finally, she said, "Great. Pick us up at eleven." She was always like that—so sure of herself. She didn't even ask if it was okay with him.

"Maybe I can give you some pointers," I said to Gideon. And Shoshanna and I started laughing. I'm completely tone deaf. Can't tell a sharp from a flat. I can't even read music.

"You probably could," Gideon said, smiling at me.

"You sure you're only sixteen?" Rafi asked.

"Joan of Arc led an army when she was my age."

"Yeah, but she had a lousy hairdo," Tamar said. "You ever see those old movies? Being a martyr is not glamorous."

I could feel a cringe shoot through everyone. Tamar had accidentally brought us back to reality. And a dark cloud suddenly hovered over the group.

"I'll give you a lift back to the dorm," Rafi said. "My mother let me borrow her car."

"See you guys," Shoshanna murmured.

"Nice to meet you," I said to the others, but it sounded hollow.

As we walked to the door, a girl hobbled in on crutches. Her right leg was missing from the knee down.

I looked away, afraid of my curiosity.

"Hey, Ruthie," Shoshanna said to her. "How you doing?"

Ruthie shrugged. "I'm coming back to school next week."

"That's great."

I sneaked a glance at Ruthie. Her face and hands looked like they had pretty much healed.

"This is my sister, Noa."

"Yeah, we met once," Ruthie said.

"At a dance," I said. Then I glanced at her crutches and flinched, embarrassed for myself and for her. I couldn't look her directly in the eyes.

People think I have a lot of nerve. Too much, maybe. But there are times when I lose that nerve. It was just so hard to look at—a victim. Maybe I didn't want to be reminded that I could be one myself.

As we walked the streets of Jerusalem towards Rafi's car, I carried my embarrassment with me. The echo of our footsteps kept reminding me of Ruthie's missing leg. I tried to concentrate on the olive trees. It's safe in this neighborhood, I kept telling myself. At least, it felt safe then.

On the short drive back to the university, I saw a young guy with a bandage wrapped around his head and another guy with an arm missing. Rafi didn't say anything. Neither did Shoshanna. I wasn't sure if she'd even seen what I saw—maybe because she was going over her music in her head, or maybe because it had become so commonplace.

I didn't notice Rafi reach over and turn on the radio. But suddenly we heard the tail end of a news broadcast: ". . . incident three hours ago in Hebron in which Israeli soldiers, who had been fired upon, shot and killed a man they believed was carrying a gun. People who witnessed the incident said the dead man, a Palestinian student at Hebrew University, did not have a weapon."

"Not again," I cried.

"High alert has been declared across the country, especially on the grounds of the university and the surrounding area."

We all snapped to attention. A wheel of anxiety turned in my stomach. I would have given anything to be sitting at home with my parents at that moment instead of riding in a car—totally exposed.

I was still feeling anxious when we got back to Shoshanna's dorm. But once we walked through the security gate, I tried to put it out of my mind.

"Rebekah decided to stay at her sister's house, so you won't have to sleep on the floor," Shoshanna said, as we walked down the corridor to her room.

That was good news. Her room was about as big as a cramped closet with two single beds. And there was barely any space between them.

"I'm sure they'll close down the campus tonight," Shoshanna said. " Because of the alert."

"You nervous?"

"It'll be okay. Security's tight here."

She put her key in the door and tried to turn it. But she couldn't. She took the key out, looked at it, and tried again.

She turned to me, confused. "There's a key in the lock. On the other side of the door. Rebekah?" she called.

No one answered.

"Weird." She tried again. The key still wouldn't work.

"Let me try," I said, taking the key from her.

I couldn't open the door either.

"Rebekah, are you in there?" she called again. She knocked on the door.

Still no answer. But we heard a sound. Both of us stopped breathing.

"Who's in there?" Shoshanna demanded.

"Shoshanna? Is that you?" a female voice asked.

Shoshanna and I looked at each other for a moment. Then Shoshanna said, "Yeah. Who are you? What are you doing in my room?"

There was a long silence. Then, "Who's with you?"

"My sister. Open the door," Shoshanna said.

The door slowly opened a crack. Two brown eyes peered out. Rebekah's eyes are green.

Shoshanna jumped back, but I pushed the door open without thinking. The girl stood there, shaking. Shoshanna was shaking, too. I didn't notice that I was until the girl drew herself together and, taking control of the moment, demanded that we shut the door. Quickly.

I started to shut the door, but Shoshanna stopped me.

"Tell me what you're doing here first," she said, challenging the girl, who was clearly an Arab.

"Rebekah said I could stay here."

Shoshanna closed the door, and she and I stood there, looking at this girl whose facial expressions traveled from self-confidence to terror and back again within a millisecond. We both silently checked out her clothes. She couldn't be hiding anything under her white shirt or black slacks. I glanced down at the bed. A black and white *kuffia*, the headscarf Palestinians sometimes wear, lay on the pillow. Her books were open. I wanted to look under the bed, but that would have been too awkward. So I just stood there thinking about the news broadcast, my mouth completely dry. And my heart thundering against my chest.

"I was studying at the library late, and I got a call on my cell phone from my mother. There's been an incident."

"We know," Shoshanna said a little too loudly. "How did you get the key to my room, and how—"

"Rebekah's in my class. She and her boyfriend were at the library, too. She said I could stay here."

"You can't stay here," Shoshanna said, quickly. "It's not allowed."

"I have no place else to go."

"Why don't you go home?" I asked.

"I can't afford to miss my classes tomorrow. And I have work to do at the library. I have a huge paper due on Sunday. I live in Abu Dis, and there's a temporary road closure between East and West Jerusalem. If I went home, I probably wouldn't be able to get back through the checkpoint in the morning," she said, her words tumbling out in a rush.

"There are two Arab girls down the hall," Shoshanna said, looking at the girl suspiciously.

"They wouldn't open their door."

"If you don't live on campus, and you're caught here, we'll both get into trouble."

"I know."

"You can't stay here. I need to call security."

"You can trust me," the girl said.

"How do I know I can trust you? You've put me in a very bad position."

Shoshanna walked over to the phone. The Arab girl and I watched her closely. Both of us were afraid of what she was going to do. But I was also torn. Part of me wanted to stop her, and part of me wanted her to call security and get that girl out of there, fast.

"Don't," I started to say. Then Shoshanna said, "Dinah," into the receiver. "Let me talk to Rebekah." The Arab girl, who had inched her way toward the door, started breathing more normally again. Shoshanna rolled her eyes. "I don't care if she's asleep. Wake her up. I need to talk to her."

Shoshanna's back was to us, but I could see the tension in her muscles. Her voice was calm, but I knew that she was pretending not to be scared for my benefit. That scared me even more. A minute later I heard her say, "Well, you should have warned me. No. No, you can't just do that. How well?" She hung up the phone.

"I have to think about this," she said to the girl. "Come on," she said to me, and we walked out of the room, leaving the girl inside.

I followed Shoshanna down the hall to Chava's room. She knocked on the door. As soon as Chava yelled, "Who is it?" we announced ourselves and scrambled in. Shoshanna whispered, "There's a strange Arab girl in my room. She doesn't live on campus."

"What!" Chava yelled. She started picking up her stuff as if she were getting ready to run.

"There was another incident. The campus is on high alert."

"I heard."

"If she goes home, she won't be able to get back here."

"Good story," Chava said, barely paying attention.

"Rebekah said she could stay in our room."

Chava dropped her books. "What! Is she crazy?"

"She said the girl's in her class, but she doesn't know her all that well."

"She is crazy."

"Maybe, but what do you think I should do?"

"Is there a question about what you should do?" Chava handed Shoshanna the phone. "Call security."

"But she's a student here."

"Yeah? Is that what you're going to say when she blows up the dorm? She wouldn't be the first female suicide bomber."

"Come on, you guys," I said. "She's not a suicide bomber."

"Oh, and what makes you such an expert?" Chava asked.

"She was more scared than we were," I said, but as I said it, I knew that Chava was right. The Arab girl wouldn't be the first female suicide bomber. Everyone was shocked when a woman from the Al-Am'ari refugee camp near Ramallah blew herself up just months before.

"You'd be scared, too, if you were going to set off a bomb," Chava shot back.

Shoshanna looked convinced. I was scared, too, even though I was pretending I wasn't. But my gut reaction was that that girl was just trying to get her schoolwork done, and it wasn't her fault that the whole country had gone completely berserk.

"Maybe we can stay in here tonight," I said to Shoshanna.

"Yeah, you can stay here because I'm going to call my parents and ask them to come for me if you don't phone security," Chava yelled.

"She's a student," I yelled back. "She was studying. Her books were on the bed."

Shoshanna thought for a moment. "Let's go back to my room," she said, finally.

"And do what?" I asked.

"Go to sleep," Shoshanna said. "Or at least try to."

We trudged back to the room, which was locked again. Shoshanna knocked lightly on the door as she identified herself.

The Arab girl opened it, and we walked in.

"You can stay here tonight, but please leave first thing in the morning," Shoshanna said.

The girl nodded her head. I could see that she was very relieved, even though she didn't bother to say so. And to tell you the truth, I was, too.

I spread my sleeping bag on the floor between the two beds and tried to go to sleep. But I just lay there for hours. Listening to the Arab girl breathe. Every time she turned, I stopped breathing. My imagination ran circles around me. I wished we had searched the closet to make sure she hadn't planted a bomb.

I started to get up, but the Arab girl moaned in her sleep, and I lay back down again, covering my head with a pillow.

By daybreak I was exhausted, and I finally fell asleep. But still, even in my sleep, I half expected the walls to come crashing down around us at any minute.

CHAPTER
2

I woke up with a start at around eight o'clock. The Arab girl was quietly opening the door, preparing to leave, just as she had promised. She glanced back quickly, and our eyes met. Then without a word she vanished.

I got up slowly and looked around the room. The Arab girl had made Rebekah's bed. Everything was in place. She hadn't left even a scrap of paper behind. But somehow the room felt different. Shoshanna must have sensed it, too. She got up, and we tip-toed around for a few minutes, feeling strange. Neither of us spoke. Then Shoshanna started rearranging her books and smoothing out the covers on her bed as if she needed to reclaim the room.

"Look—I know it's not easy for you to keep a secret," Shoshanna said, as we started getting dressed. "But I don't think you should tell Mom and Dad about the Arab girl."

"You think I'm crazy? They'd never let me out of the house again. You did the right thing," I said. "Not calling security."

"Maybe."

I sat through Shoshanna's classes pretending that I understood the lectures. But to tell you the truth, I was bored out of my mind, and I was daydreaming about meeting her friends again for dinner. One friend in particular. But that night the campus was still on high alert, and everyone was "strongly discouraged" from leaving. Some of the students scaled the walls. But after our experience the night before, we decided just to scrounge around in Shoshanna's little refrigerator. Actually, she decided. I'd have jumped the wall in a minute. We came up with yogurt and fruit for dinner. Then we went to the common area on her floor and hung out with some other girls from her dorm.

Shoshanna is not the talkative type, so she didn't mention a word about the Arab girl to the other girls sitting around with us. And Chava wasn't there. But two minutes into a conversation with Tamar, I blurted it out. Suddenly, there was complete chaos. Everybody started talking at once, and the opinions flew around so fast, I couldn't catch all of them. "Call security right now!" "It's over. Forget it!" "You could have put us all in jeopardy!" "Okay, so you did the right thing!" "You didn't check her ID? That's not so smart." My head whipped around as I looked from one girl to another, and I jumped right into the conversation myself sometimes.

Still, since we felt relatively safe in the dorm, it was kind of exciting talking about all the possibilities. Like telling ghost stories around a camp fire.

By the next morning, the high alert was called off. Gideon picked us up in his mother's car and drove us to his house. It would have been easier to take the bus, but in Jerusalem there are no buses on the Jewish Sabbath, between sundown on Friday and sundown on Saturday. And though that usually makes me crazy, for once it was just fine with me. Having to wait at the bus stop on such a sweltering day was not my idea of a good time. But getting to ride in a car with Gideon was, even if I did have to sit in the back seat.

About a half hour into the rehearsal, I was sorry I'd suggested coming along. How many times can you listen to Bach's Concerto for Violin and Cello played over and over again? I was glad I'd brought some of my schoolwork with me. Even looking at Gideon was not enough to keep me awake.

Finally, I decided to poke around the house, which had been built one hundred years ago and has arched doorways and tile floors. I started to wonder whose house it had been and why the owner had left. There are stories. All kinds of stories. I don't like to believe them, but it's better to know the truth than to hide your head in the sand. The thing is, sometimes it's hard to know whose truth to listen to.

Shoshanna and Gideon finally finished practicing, and we sat down on the patio to eat the lunch that Gideon's mother had left for us—hummus (which is made from ground chickpeas), eggplant salad, chopped tomatoes and cucumbers, olives, yogurt, and pita bread.

The bougainvillea that twined around the fence was in bloom, and the day suddenly felt magical. We joked around and laughed, and it seemed at that moment as if we were safe and warm and totally invulnerable.

"Noa's on the debate team," Shoshanna told Gideon.

"That's because I'm the only one in the family who can't play a musical instrument," I admitted. "The only way I could get any attention was by talking louder and faster than my sister and brother."

"Oh, I bet you'd do that even if you could play a musical instrument," Gideon said.

"Yeah, you're right."

"And she's a great athlete," Shoshanna said. "She placed second in the Maccabee fifty yard dash last year. Of course, she has the longest legs in the family, too."

"What are you trying to do, Shosh? Marry me off?"

Everyone started to laugh. But I was kind of embarrassed. I couldn't believe I'd actually said that.

"Sounds like a good idea," Gideon said.

"So, are you available?" I asked. It had slipped out of my mouth before I could stop it.

"For you—I'm always available."

Yeah, sure, I thought. If only that were true.

The day got away from us. Suddenly, it was almost sundown. The buses would be running soon. And my parents were expecting me to take the first bus home. We piled into Gideon's car and headed back toward the dorm so I could get my stuff.

Gideon drove past the Old City, the area of Jerusalem that is surrounded by a high, thick wall. Like a fortress. I glanced over at the Jaffa Gate. We used to shop inside before the current Arab uprising. What the Arabs call the intifada. We can still go into the Jewish Quarter if we want to, but we aren't really welcome in the Arab Quarter now.

This war between us, which isn't called a war, is hard on everyone. The Arabs in the Old City don't want us to come there any more. And I guess I can understand why. It's a really complicated situation. And everyone has a different point of view. What's the truth? It depends on who you ask.

By the time Shoshanna and I got to the bus stop, it was already lined with people ready to push and shove their way onto the bus, as if they thought the first five to board would get some kind of prize. Or maybe it's just that Israelis have a different sense of time. In a world where you never know for sure if you're going to survive once you walk out your front door, every minute counts.

"So, thanks," I said to Shosh. "I had a great time."

"Me, too. And so did Gideon. I think he likes you."

"Really?"

"Really."

"Not likes me, likes me, though, huh?"

"I'm not sure."

"Tell him even though I'm only sixteen chronologically, I'm eighteen in my soul."

"I'll tell him. Not that it matters. He has a short attention span when it comes to girls, if you know what I mean."

"You mean by the time I get back to Beit Zeit, he'll have forgotten about me."

"Possibly."

"Speaking of Beit Zeit, are you coming home first, or are you going to meet us in Netanya for Passover?"

"I'll come home first. Mom wants us all to drive up together."

Just then the Egged bus pulled up. Shaul, the father of my best friend, Sarah, was the driver. Even though the campus had been taken off high alert, my parents had wanted to pick me up, but I had begged them not to. I wanted to hold onto those last delicious moments of independence. Not that my parents hover over me all the time, but I'm sure they would have insisted on coming for me if I'd told them about the Arab girl.

Most of the passengers were already seated when I climbed on the bus. I sat down in back of Shaul and watched him. As he took people's money, he checked out everyone wearing baggy clothes or carrying a bag where explosives could be concealed. Well, to be honest—not everyone. He was checking out anyone who looked like an Arab, but he was trying to be as subtle as possible.

See, there's this automatic fear that sort of washes over us before our brains kick in. The moment we start thinking rationally, we calm down and tell ourselves that most Palestinians are people just like us. But still, in the backs of our minds, we're thinking, could this Palestinian or that Palestinian be a suicide bomber? Then we feel guilty for thinking like that. And we feel embarrassed for ourselves and embarrassed for them.

So I kind of figured that's what was going on with Shaul. I felt safe in Shaul's hands. "I'm not scared. It's my job," he told me once. But I know Sarah's mother has been trying to get him to quit.

Just as the bus was about to take off, a dark-skinned guy who was acting a little nervous got on. I saw the tension in Shaul's shoulders. My stomach muscles tightened, and panic flooded through me. I quickly looked around the bus. Everyone else was on alert, too. I grabbed the sides of my seat and held my breath as if that would stop time. And, in fact, it seemed to. It took forever for Shaul to lift his hand in slow motion and ask the guy for ID. There's a fine line between being cautious and making a potential suicide bomber even more nervous.

Then the guy looked at Shaul hard. Shaul stared back at him, not exactly challenging him, but, with a steady, silent gaze, compelling him to surrender. The guy reached into his pants' pocket as he started to speak. And we all felt the tension drain out of us. We could tell by his accent that he was a Moroccan Jew, not an Arab.

"This is the first time I've been on a bus since my wife—"

The man couldn't finish his sentence.

CHAPTER
3

Beit Zeit, where I live, is in the hills just outside of Jerusalem, carved into the Jerusalem Forest. It's beautiful and quiet—too quiet for me. But there's space here. In the city, most people live in apartments with just a few rooms. We have some land and trees, lots and lots of old, old olive trees. That's what Beit Zeit means. House of Olives.

I was tired by the time I trudged up to the door. When I opened it, I heard voices coming from the kitchen, where everybody gathers. I recognized the voices immediately. My mother's, my father's, and those of our friends Abed and Dahlia. Abed lives in Abu Gosh, an Arab village not far from here. He's a doctor with a private practice, but he does a lot of volunteer work in the territories. Dahlia's a doctor, too, only she works at Hadassah Hospital.

As I edged closer to our kitchen, I realized they were talking politics, as usual. And as usual they seemed to agree. The conversations between my parents and Abed and Dahlia always ended with one of them saying, "Unless both the Palestinians and the Israelis are willing to compromise, there will never be peace. They—we—have to keep talking. Otherwise the situation is hopeless."

"I'm here," I announced, as I walked into the room.

Abed got up and gave me a hug. "You're growing up too fast," he said.

"Not fast enough," I said back to him.

Everybody laughed.

"So how was your weekend?" my mother asked.

"Great."

"What did you do?"

Even though I'd promised Shoshanna not to say anything, I started to tell them about the Arab girl in Shoshanna's room. Suddenly, I froze. I looked at Abed self-consciously. "Shoshanna took me to meet her friends, and they were so cool. I think they liked me," I said instead.

"I'm sure they did," my father said.

"So, how many babies did you deliver this week?" I asked Dahlia, trying to divert the attention away from me.

Three

"Eight," she said proudly. "Eight big, fat, healthy babies."

"Are you two ever going to get married and have your own babies?"

Abed laughed. "Maybe when we're old enough to be grandparents," he said, and he glanced at Dahlia.

Dahlia's not exactly the blushing type. She grew up on a kibbutz, and she's smart and tough and pretty edgy. But for a moment, the color rose to her cheeks, and it looked as if she wasn't sure whether she wanted to laugh or cry. I knew I'd blurted out the wrong question, and I could feel the heat rising to my cheeks, as well.

"I gotta finish my homework," I said, quickly. "I'll talk to you later."

I walked through the kitchen and could see the olive trees in the lower yard. They looked like shadows waving their arms in the air. A shiver went through me, and I hurried into the living room with its high-pitched ceiling. It's a big, beautiful room with a fireplace surrounded by couches, Oriental rugs, book shelves, and paintings on the walls. In a corner is a colorful old camel bag woven thick with wool of many colors. My father bought it from an Arab vendor in the Old City many years ago. It reminds me of the coat Jacob gave to his favorite son, Joseph.

As soon as I entered the hallway that links the old part of the house with this part, the air changed. The hallway was once a chicken coop. I sniffed the mold we can never get rid of, no matter how hard we scrub. This was the original part of the house, and leaks keep springing up. Its low ceilings are oppressive, and the rooms are dark, so I didn't usually spend much time in it. I liked to study at the kitchen table. But as it was being occupied, I knew I'd have to work in my room, the room I used to share with Shoshanna.

My brother Ari's room is the first one on the left. He wasn't home very often then because he was in the army, officially the Israeli Defense Force. Everybody calls it the IDF. But he sometimes got leave to come home on weekends. I heard him playing his guitar that night, and I checked my watch. He should be heading back to base by now, I thought.

I knocked on the door, and he stopped playing. "That you, Noa?" he asked.

"It's me," I said, as I walked into his room, which was a mess. His clothes were in a heap on the floor, and his guitar case was sitting on top of them. He put his guitar down and looked at me. There was something wrong. I could tell right away.

CHAPTER
4

A ri ran his hand through his short hair, which is dark like mine. We look alike. At a glance you can tell that we're related. He's tall and slender, like I am. We have dark skin, like my father's side of the family, who've lived in Israel for five generations. Not dark, dark, but sort of light olive. Shoshanna is really light-skinned, like my mother's side of the family. That grandfather was from Germany—but that's another story—and that grandmother was from France.

"What's up?" I asked. "Aren't you supposed to be heading back to base?"

"Yeah," he said. "I have to get going."

But he didn't move.

"Dad going to drive you? Or are you taking the bus?"

"I need to talk to Mom and Dad before I go back."

"Abed and Dahlia are in there with them."

"I know. That's why I'm waiting."

I wished Ari would just tell me what was going on instead of forcing me to pull it out of him.

"So why didn't you talk to Mom and Dad yesterday? Something just come up?"

"No, it's just that—"

"What?" I blurted out. "Did you get a girl pregnant, or something?"

He smiled. "I wish."

"So?"

"My unit's been assigned to Hebron."

"Oh no," I shrieked. Then, horrified, I covered my mouth.

I slumped down on Ari's bed. "That's terrible. I mean, that's—I know how you feel about patrolling the territories. I mean, what if—"

"I'm not going. I've decided to refuse service in the West Bank."

My mouth dropped open, and I was speechless for a moment, which is unusual for me.

"You'll go to jail," I finally stammered.

"Yeah, maybe," my brother said. My brother, who can't stand closed places. Who has to sleep with his windows open even when it's raining. Who pushed for moving out of our apartment in Jerusalem and living in the hills so he could walk out the door and be free.

"You're really willing to go to jail?"

"I don't have a choice. It's all so crazy. I can't go into Hebron. I don't want to kill someone accidentally—some kid, maybe. The invincible Israeli Defense Force. Defense! That's what we're *supposed* to do—defend. Not attack. I can't do it."

"I'm glad," I said, slowly. "If you could, you wouldn't be you."

He smiled at me gently. "Thanks. It's not going to be easy for you—not when the other kids find out."

"Who cares?" I asked, a little too loudly. "If they don't think it's cool, they're not people I want to hang out with, anyway."

Just then we heard the front door close, and Mom and Dad said good-bye to Abed and Dahlia. I looked at Ari. He breathed deeply. Then he let his breath out in a long, protracted sigh. I wanted to take his hand, go with him when he left the room, but I knew that this was something he had to do alone.

Ari turned and looked at me when he got to the door. I knew what he was thinking. Once he told our parents, it was a done deal. There would be no turning back. I gave him a thumbs up. But as I listened to his footsteps echoing down the hallway, I realized that my hands were shaking.

CHAPTER
5

My mother went with my father when he drove Ari back to his army base that night, and then they came home and went straight to their room. We were all rushing around in the morning, so there was no mention of Ari's decision. But I'd been burning up with it all day. I'd be answering a question in English class, and it would remind me somehow of Ari. And my heart would start to pound. I'd want to just yell out, this is so unimportant. Who cares if you use "lay" or "lie"? Everyone knows what you mean. It's not a matter of life or death, is it? I wanted to discuss what is morally right and wrong, not grammar.

My problem was, if I didn't talk about something that bothered me, I couldn't let go of it. And I imagined that it was far worse than it really was. So it was hard to concentrate in school that day, and I was glad when classes were over. My best friend, Sarah, and I walked into the bright sunshine and shivered with freedom. Homework could wait for a few hours. We decided to ditch our books and hike into the Jerusalem Forest.

I wanted to tell Sarah about Ari and about the Arab girl. Even then, the two things seemed related somehow. I started talking as soon as we hit the trail. If you can't tell your best friend how you feel, who can you tell?

"Ari was home for the weekend," I said.

"I saw him walk past my house on Saturday. I bet he looks so totally cool in his uniform."

"Yeah," I said, and I didn't know why, but I was suddenly nervous about telling her. "He was probably going hiking."

"My dad told me you were on his route Saturday night."

"I sat right in back of him, like I always do."

"It's the safest place unless a nut case sits in back of you, puts a bomb under your seat, and detonates it with a cell phone."

"Like in Tel Aviv," I said. But even as I said it, it didn't seem real to me. Even though Tel Aviv is a less than an hour's drive from here, the incident seemed remote. It felt no more real than the incidents that had taken place right here in Jerusalem. Buses had blown up. Bombs had been detonated at the open vegetable market, school yards had been targeted, cafés and dance halls destroyed. But at that point in my life, I'd never been there when it happened. And I'd never been really close to anyone who'd been killed. Even though I felt really sorry for those people and their families—in truth—I never really knew how they felt. I just thought I did.

Sometimes when I'd walk past a place where there'd been a bombing, and only the ghost of it remained, my knees would get weak, and I'd realize that I could have been there when it happened. But I wasn't. So the reality slipped through my fingers like a bad dream and left only an uncomfortable feeling.

"It was terrible," Sarah said. She frowned, and her whole face collapsed into a wrinkle. I almost envy Sarah. She has the ability to feel pain deep down in her soul. Anybody's pain, not just hers. This also ticked me off about her. Sometimes I just wanted to say, "Get a grip, girl. Move on. Save your tears for someone you love."

"The good thing about that incident is that nobody was killed," I said, trying to sound optimistic. Or maybe I was just being contrary.

"Tell that to the girl who lost her legs."

"I feel safe with your dad driving, though."

"Yeah, well, I don't feel like he's very safe. But he thinks it's his duty. It's his way of being patriotic, I guess."

"What do you mean?"

"Well, his reserve unit obviously isn't going to be sent to the Gaza Strip or Hebron. They're way too old."

I swallowed hard. I was beginning to get the feeling that Sarah and I might not have the same opinion about Ari's choice. But I was thinking I could convince her to see it my way. She's pretty stubborn, but she's usually reasonable. Still, I wasn't quite sure how to bring it up. Then I said to myself—hey, what's going on here? Since when do you censor yourself? And without even waiting for an answer, I totally changed the subject.

"I'm in love," I said.

Sarah stopped walking and looked at me as if I'd suddenly lost my mind. She's short, with short, bluntly cut black hair, and she's a little on the chunky side. So when she puts her hands on her hips and rolls her eyes, she reminds me of one of those wooden dolls we used to play with when we were kids. I bit my bottom lip and looked away from her.

"You're in love? You're not even hanging out with anyone special. At least not that I know of, and if I don't know, then you're not, so how can you suddenly be in love, and who's it with, anyway?" she said in a burst of disbelief and surprise.

I laughed. "You can't tell anyone."

"Who would I tell?"

"Should I start naming names?"

"Just tell me," she yelled, and her voice echoed through the woods. "Tell me, tell me, tell me."

"Gideon."

"Who?"

"Gideon. The guy who plays the cello with my sister."

"Oh him."

"What's that supposed to mean?" I asked, indignantly.

"It means, is this another one of your fantasy boyfriends?"

"Okay, maybe," I admitted. "So who doesn't daydream about guys? At least, my fantasies might become realities. I don't dream about movie stars or singers. I dream about real people."

Sarah laughed. "You have about as much chance of hooking up with Gideon as you do of going out with Justin Timberlake."

"How can you say that? I've never met Justin Timberlake. I was at Gideon's house!"

"Alone?"

"With my sister. We had lunch at his house, and he talked to me a lot. Shoshanna said he likes me."

"You sure he doesn't like Shoshanna?"

"No. I mean, yes. Well, you know, she's not interested in him. Except as a musician. She doesn't have time for guys."

"If I were as cool as your sister, I wouldn't have time for anything else."

"She's really serious about her music."

"Lucky you," Sarah said, and I detected a slight touch of envy. "If your sister's not interested in him, maybe you have a chance."

"I mean, I'm not sure he likes me, but he is so hot, Sarah. I could really, really like him."

"So, maybe he does like you," Sarah conceded, good-naturedly. "If you do go out with him, will you ask him if he has a friend?"

"It's probably just a fantasy," I said.

Sarah shrugged her shoulders. "You never know. So will you ask him?"

"Deal."

"Really?"

"Really. You're my best friend, so why wouldn't I ask him? I'm not exactly shy about those things."

"You're not shy about anything," Sarah said, laughing. "Remember what you did in algebra class last year?"

"Which thing?"

"I'm thinking about the time the teacher showed the class how to solve a really hard problem, which no one could get, and you insisted that you had another way of doing it."

"Oh yeah. I remember that."

"Boy, did he get upset."

"Well, I was right."

"No, you weren't."

"We got the same answer, didn't we?"

"I guess so, but how could you know more than the teacher? It was just luck that the answers came out the same."

"There's no such thing as luck in math. That's what's so beautiful about it. There are only right answers and wrong answers."

"I never thought about it that way."

"That's why I like it. It's precise. Not like life in Israel where nothing's just black or white."

"Oh, come on. You can't mean that."

"Of course I do."

"Nothing?"

"Okay. Murder. You should never kill anyone under any circumstances. Period."

"Well, maybe that's not exactly true," Sarah said. "I mean what if you're defending yourself or your children?"

"Yeah, I guess, but then it's not murder exactly."

"Or what if you're defending your country?"

"Okay. I get where you're going. But that's different. It's a lot more complicated. I mean, would you consider the killing of innocent people who just happen to be in the wrong place at the wrong time murder?"

"Oh," she said, quietly. "That's a tough question."

"We do that, sometimes," I said, hesitantly.

"What?"

"Accidentally kill innocent civilians."

"Yeah, but they shouldn't be shielding terrorists," she said, defiantly.

"How can you prove that they're shielding terrorists?" I asked, raising my voice.

"Well, it's hard to prove sometimes."

"Exactly."

"So, what are we supposed to do? Just let these terrorists get away with it? I mean, how many more Israelis have to die?"

"Ari's in jail," I blurted out.

This didn't compute for Sarah. She just looked at me.

"He couldn't do it," I said, and I knew she didn't have any idea what I was talking about. She just shook her head in disbelief.

I picked up a stick on the path and started poking the ground with it.

"He told us last night. His unit's being sent to Hebron, and he's refusing to go."

Sarah's mouth dropped open. "He can't do that."

"That's what I said."

"I mean, how could he?"

"He's probably in a military prison right now."

"That's not what I mean. I mean how could he be so unpatriotic? If everyone refused to serve in the territories, the terrorists would just go in and blow up all the Jewish settlers."

"Let the settlers police themselves," I said. "No one forced them to move into the territories." The minute I said it, I knew how stupid it sounded, but, in a way, I meant it.

"How can you say that?" Sarah asked, and she looked like she was going to cry. "No soldiers at the checkpoints. The terrorists could just cross over into settlements whenever they want to."

"Well, maybe we shouldn't have any settlements in Hebron, anyway," I insisted. "It's their town. It was their town for hundreds of years before the Six Day War."

"It was ours first," she said, holding her ground.

"In biblical times? How far back are we supposed to go? Should the United States give California back to Mexico? It was part of Mexico less than two hundred years ago. Or maybe they should give the whole country back to the Indians."

"You're arguing my point," Sarah said, and I could see she was getting angry, but so was I. "The United States won the war. No one asked them to give California back. You don't hear about Mexican suicide bombers making videotapes saying that they're killing themselves because they want to be martyrs for their country. We won the war. We need the territories for security. It's simple."

"I've never heard you talk like that," I said to Sarah.

"Well, I've been thinking about it," she said. "Every day when my dad leaves for work, I think about it. I think what if he doesn't come home? What if his bus is a target? I don't care about Palestinians anymore. They hate us. And what do we do? We stand out in the streets like idiots and carry peace signs."

"If no one wants peace," I yelled, "then there'll never be any hope. So what if Yasir Arafat doesn't really want it? Lots of Palestinians do. There's still hope, Sarah."

"For what?" she asked, belligerently, as she kicked a rock out of the way.

"For this to end," I said, quietly.

"And in the meantime, if every soldier did what your brother is doing, it would mean the end of us," she said. And she got up and started walking on ahead of me.

CHAPTER

6

Sarah and I didn't say another word to each other. I knew she kept waiting for me to tell her she was right, and I kept waiting for her to admit that I was right. But when we reached my house, she just muttered, "See you," and she kept walking. I couldn't believe it.

Sarah's parents must have been talking about the war a lot, I decided, and she was just repeating what she had heard. Of course, I guess I was, more or less, repeating what my parents had said, as well. Whose parents weren't talking about the war? Hardly a day went by when we weren't, in some way, reminded of it.

Well, that's not exactly true. Sometimes a week or two would pass without an incident. Sometimes a month or two. Then without commenting on it, we'd all begin to relax a little, pretend that we live in a normal country. Nobody says anything. As if talking about it will jinx it, which is ridiculous because we're jinxed anyway.

Why can't life be more like math? I asked myself as I strode into the kitchen for dinner. Math was so clear-cut, unlike the war. I wondered what the Arab girl would say if she were telling the story of this war. Her version would be very different from mine, and from Sarah's. I decided not to call Sarah, but to let her call me. We always did our chemistry homework together, and she sometimes got stuck, so I would help her out. She helped me with English when I had trouble with the poetry assignments. Though I can speak English pretty well, analyzing poetry used to drive me crazy, but it was easy for Sarah. That night, we didn't have an English assignment, so I figured she would be the one to call me.

Just then I remembered that I didn't get to tell Sarah—or anyone else—about the Arab girl. And it was such a great story.

"Wash the tomatoes," my mother said. "Then cut up the cucumbers."

"Do I have to?"

"What am I? Your servant? Of course, you have to," my mother said, laughing.

My mother's good mood irritated me. How could she be in a good mood given the present circumstances?

I washed the tomatoes from our garden and chopped them; then I started attacking the cucumbers. Wielding the knife relaxed me a little. Not a lot, but enough to be semi-civil.

"Sarah's pissed at me," I said, as I continued chopping.

"How come?"

"Because she doesn't know what she's talking about," I said.

"So you're pissed at her, too."

"I didn't say that."

"Ummmm," my mother said, as she mashed the eggplant.

"I told her about Ari," I said, without looking up at her.

"Ummmm," my mother responded, with a slightly different tilt, as if she were trying to sing the right notes to an unfamiliar tune.

"She thinks what he's doing is terrible."

"I'm sorry," my mother said.

"About what?" I asked, confused. Was she sorry that Ari had refused to serve in Hebron, or was she sorry that Sarah and I had had an argument?

"I'm sorry that Sarah disappointed you."

"It's just that she wouldn't listen to me. And this is important, and she should listen to me."

"You can't force people to agree with you. You can only state your arguments and hope they understand."

"That is so rational," I yelled. I hadn't meant to yell, but I hate it when she talks like that—when she's being more rational than I am.

My mother stopped mashing the eggplant and looked as if she'd like to pick up the dish and throw it at me. In a way, I wished she would have. She didn't, of course. She's much too reasonable.

Just then, my father walked in, kissed both of us on our cheeks, and washed his hands.

"How are my girls?" he asked.

"A little testy," my mother answered.

"Speak for yourself," I said, under my breath.

"Maybe everybody's hungry," my father, the appeaser, said.

We sat down at the table, and I was feeling very cranky. I could feel the fidgets building up inside of me. I recognized the symptoms. They usually get me into trouble. When I was little I spent many time-outs in my room, thinking about what I had said or done that had driven everyone crazy.

"Sarah seems to be upset about Ari's decision," my mother told my father.

"I don't want to talk about it," I said, angrily.

My father raised his hands slightly and cocked his head to the side to let me know that he understood.

"Noa," my mother said, "not everybody's going to understand why Ari decided to refuse service in Hebron. The important thing is whether you understand what he's doing and why."

"You think I'm a baby, or something? Of course, I understand. Do *you*?" I shot back.

"Look, I know this isn't easy for you, but you're going to have to talk to me civilly," my mother said.

"Fine," I muttered.

"And I mean civilly."

"I understand what he's doing," I said, "but I'm worried about him."

My mother and father exchanged looks.

"We are, too," my father said.

"He's not in solitary confinement," my mother said, as if this would make it okay. "He's in detention. A military prison isn't so horrible, and it's probably only for a short time. We've already talked to a lawyer. He thought that after a month or so Ari might be given a chance to change his mind. He doesn't think the army wants the kind of publicity a court martial would bring."

"Yeah, well, I don't think he's going to change his mind. And I don't think I'd like to be locked up for a month," I said.

"This is his choice," my mother said, quietly, "and we have to honor it."

"Well, I want everybody else to honor it, too," I said, even more quietly.

My father nodded, but there was a certain sadness in his eyes. "It's hard to buck the system, especially the military system. It's hard to do what you think is morally right when everyone else thinks you're wrong."

I went back to my room after dinner and flopped down on my bed. All my thoughts were jumbled up, and the stories of the day kept bumping into each other.

I lay there waiting, waiting for Sarah to call about the chemistry homework. But the phone remained silent.

CHAPTER

7

Sarah and I avoided each other all the next day. Of course, we pretended we weren't really avoiding each other. We pretended we didn't see each other. We were careful not to make eye contact in the classes we had together. We both laughed with other friends. We both have lots of friends, but usually we were together, with or without our other friends.

I don't know if anyone noticed or not. I wasn't going to say anything about our argument, but I wondered if Sarah would. And I wondered if she'd tell our friends about Ari.

By the time we got to chemistry class, the last period of the day, I couldn't wait to see if she'd turn in her homework. She didn't. I gloated for a minute. Then I felt sorry for her. She'd probably wanted to call me for help. I sat in class the whole time wondering if I should go up to her and offer to help her, pretend nothing was wrong between us. We used to get mad at each other when we were in first grade, but we never stayed mad for more than fifteen minutes, so our not talking that morning felt very strange and uncomfortable. One thing, though, neither of us liked to apologize.

But since *she* was the one who hadn't shown any respect for what *my* brother chose to do, *I* didn't think I should be the one to go up to her. At the same time, deep down I realized that I hadn't shown much respect for the danger her father faced every day when he drove his bus. I decided to walk up to her after class and suggest that maybe we were both wrong. Then I'd ask her if she wanted to come over to my house so we could do our homework together.

"You better start taking notes," said Matti, my lab partner.

"Oh," I said, startled. I picked up my pencil and tried to listen to Mr. Drucker, but my mind kept wandering. I kept thinking about Ari.

"My brother's a refusenik," I whispered to Matti.

Matti turned to look at me. "You're kidding!"

"No, he is."

"How can he be a refusenik? I thought he was already in the army. He didn't refuse to sign up for the draft."

"Yeah, that's true. But he refuses to serve in the territories."

"Wow!"

I waited for him to say something else, but he didn't. And Mr. Drucker—the only teacher in Israel who insisted that we call him mister—was staring at me, so I couldn't say anything else, either.

When the class ended, I picked up my books slowly and started heading toward Sarah, but she walked around the other way and called out to Aviva. Then she and Aviva went off, laughing together. I just stood there for a moment, watching them. Then I bit my lower lip until it really hurt and shoved my books into my book bag.

"Hey," Matti said, "I'm going horseback riding. Come with me."

"I don't have a horse," I said, morosely.

"Whose horse is that I see in your backyard sometimes?"

"A friend's." I didn't mention Abed's name because I didn't want Matti to give me an "are you out of your mind" look because my family has an Arab friend.

"So we can go over to Shlomo's."

We both took riding lessons from Shlomo, who has a stable in Beit Zeit. We can ride pretty well. But personally I had other things on my mind. And I hadn't ridden for a while, so I hesitated.

"You're coming," Matti insisted.

At that moment, I looked out the window and saw Sarah and Aviva leave school together. "Sure. Why not?" I said.

We rode in the hills toward the valley of Ein Karem, and it was a typically perfect Jerusalem day. Warm but not humid. The sun was friendly, not like it is when there's a *hamsin*, a hot, dry wind off the desert, which fries your skin and makes you want to jump out of it. Even the nights are hot then. But that day the sun just lingered, turning the mountains red. Lizards and grasshoppers scurried across our path, and the sage growing beside it had flowered. The smell mingled with the smell of my horse, and I breathed in their strong odors.

I looked down at Beit Zeit. We'd come a long way up, and I could see all the little roads weaving around houses grouped together into their own mini-neighborhoods. I saw our house. I could see Sarah's house, too. If I could just keep riding, I thought I'd be perfectly happy. I'd ridden this horse many times in the past. We had an understanding. I barely had to touch her, and she knew what I wanted.

I love horses. As soon as I learned to ride, I wanted to gallop and jump. I even ride bareback sometimes. Then you really get close to the horse. If I weren't so tall, I'd consider being a jockey. Not that we have jockeys in Israel. But I could go to the United States, I guess.

Seven

If I went to the United States, I'd want to live someplace quiet. Not near a big city or a sea port. Not near any tall buildings. The thing is, you can get away from the center of things in the United States. Here—everything's a target.

Matti and I took the horses back. Then we started walking toward my house. I'd known Matti all my life, but suddenly he was acting weird. Like he wanted to hold my hand, or put his arm around me. I was not attracted to Matti. No way. Still, I liked him, and I didn't want to hurt his feelings, so I pretended I didn't notice, and I lifted my hand to scratch my nose.

"I was visiting my sister at Hebrew University last weekend," I said. "It's so cool there."

"Yeah, I bet."

"I can't wait to graduate. I just hope my grades are good enough to get in."

"What do you have, one 2?"

"Mostly 1s. A few 2s in English and algebra," I said.

"Oh yeah. Algebra," he said, and he laughed. "You're lucky you didn't flunk that class. The teacher hated you."

"He didn't hate me," I said, indignantly.

"Yeah, he did."

"No, he didn't, Matti."

"I heard you gave him a nervous breakdown."

"Come on."

"Seriously. He didn't come back this year, did he?"

For a minute, I was stunned. I hadn't meant to literally drive him crazy. I was just showing off. Then I remembered. "He's in the army, weirdo."

Matti slapped his leg and laughed so loudly I wanted to give him a shove.

"Almost had you," he said.

"Yeah, but you didn't."

Sixteen-year-old guys are totally still little boys. Gideon would never have acted like this, I thought.

"So, does your sister have a boyfriend?" he asked, like he was reading my mind.

"Not really."

"Well, you can tell her I'm available."

"I'll be sure to do that," I said, sarcastically. "I think she's been waiting around for you to call."

"You sure you're not the one who's been waiting around for me to call?"

"Yeah, I've been glued to the phone," I said, moving away from him.

"Just kidding," he said.

I was glad we were almost to my house, which we were approaching from the back. The crickets were already chirping, and I could see Isaac, my huge land turtle, making his way across the patio toward his dinner.

"I'd do it, too," Matti said, suddenly.

"Do it?" I asked. I had no idea what he was talking about.

"Refuse to guard the settlements. Tell your brother I think he's cool."

I listened to the crickets for a minute. Then I leaned over and kissed Matti on the cheek. "Thanks for walking me home," I said.

Matti was so shocked, he just stood there for a moment. Then he said, "See you."

"See you," I said, and I opened the patio door and slipped into the house.

CHAPTER

8

"Sarah called," my mother said when I walked into the kitchen. I made a mad dash for the phone, carried it into my room, and shut the door, though my mother couldn't possibly have heard my conversation from that far away.

"Hi," I said, casually, when Sarah answered the phone.

There was a long pause, and I knew right away that something was wrong.

"My mom said you called."

"I didn't call," she said.

"But my mom said—"

"I didn't call," she said, decisively.

"Oh."

There was another long pause.

"Okay, then," I said. "See you."

"See you," she said, and we both hung up.

I was shocked. I didn't know what kind of game Sarah was playing, but it was truly out of character for her.

My shock drifted into confusion—and hurt.

What were Sarah and Aviva giggling about after school? Sarah had probably told Aviva we had a fight. We'd been best friends all of our lives; we didn't keep even one secret from each other and suddenly we weren't speaking because of politics! How crazy was that?

I wanted to call her back, tell her she didn't need a new best friend. I was still her best friend. At least, I hoped I was. I wanted to tell her that it isn't easy knowing your brother's rotting away in jail. I wanted to tell her that I was upset because, regardless of her feelings about the army, I expected her to understand my feelings. And I wanted to tell her I was sorry I hadn't understood hers.

I picked up the phone and started to dial her number. Then I put it down again. If she had wanted to talk to me, she'd had the chance. I had just called her, hadn't I? And she'd just been really, really rude to me. I decided to wait for her to call me and when she did, I'd tell her all of this, and I'd say it really politely. Then she'd be

31

upset that she had hurt my feelings, and I would tell her I was sorry I had hurt hers. But in the meantime, I still felt angry, which is much easier than feeling hurt.

"Mom," I yelled, as I walked out of my room.

The coffee grinder was going, and she didn't hear me. I yelled "Mom" again anyway.

I walked into the kitchen and tapped her on the shoulder. "Sarah did not call me," I said, accusingly.

"Did I say 'Sarah'?"

"Yeah."

"I meant Shoshanna," she said, as she started taking stuff out of the refrigerator for dinner.

"You meant Shoshanna?" I yelled.

My mother turned and looked at me.

"What's the big deal?" she asked.

"What's the big deal? Maybe I didn't want to talk to Sarah right now."

"Well, you ran out of here like you couldn't wait to call her."

She started washing the tomatoes. I rolled my eyes. "Forget it," I said. I didn't feel like going into it then, so I started to walk away.

"We're all a little preoccupied, Noa," she said, by way of an explanation.

"Yeah," I said, and all the anger seeped out of me. "Did you hear from him? Can we see him or talk to him?" I started to picture my brother going nuts in his cell, standing there rattling the bars like they do in prison movies.

"Not yet," she said. And I could see that she was pretending to be less upset than she was. "But we can call him tomorrow, and he'll be able to call us."

"Did you tell Mimi?" My grandmother insisted that we call her Mimi. She couldn't stand *safta*, the Hebrew word for grandmother. She said it made her feel like a stuffed animal.

"No. I haven't told her yet."

"You have to tell her before we go to Netanya for Passover."

"I know."

"If Ari doesn't show up, she'll know something's wrong, and she'll be pissed that you didn't tell her."

"Maybe he'll be out of prison by then."

"Are you kidding? Passover's only four weeks away."

I knew why my mother didn't want to tell Mimi about Ari. When Ari went into the army, Mimi was thrilled. It was during the lull between the first and second uprisings, so he didn't think he'd have to face what he's facing now. He didn't exactly go in willingly, but he went, just like we all do after high school graduation, just like Shoshanna had. But we didn't really worry about her. She had had an office job.

Ari could have declared himself a conscientious objector, I guess. There were a few conscientious objectors, and there were a group of refuseniks, guys who had refused to sign up for the draft in the first place. It was not such a big deal then. But now it's a different story. The army has been coming down hard on the refuseniks, keeping them in prison for much longer.

Even if Ari were given the chance to change his mind, I was sure he would still refuse to serve in the territories, so there was no way he was going to get out for Passover. And there was no way that Mimi was going to take his refusal to guard Hebron lightly. Mimi might have weighed only one hundred pounds, but she was a tough old bird. "A soldier's duty is to defend his country," she told Ari when he complained about how humiliating it would be if he had to check people at border crossings.

Mimi thought that the army was a great career move. She pointed out that Ariel Sharon, our prime minister, had been a general. Every time she said this Ari looked like he was going to puke.

I wish Ari had just left the country instead of going into the army. People do that. My parents offered to send him to the United States to study, but he said it was his duty to go. He just didn't think it was his duty to defend and protect Jewish settlers who claim they have more right to the land than the Palestinians who live there.

"I'm so sick of all this," I yelled.

"We all are," my mother said.

I slumped down at the round, wooden table my father had made for us, and I ran my hand over the smooth surface. I sighed. It would be a long time until the whole family sat around this table again, I thought. What I didn't know was that it would be much longer than I could ever have imagined.

CHAPTER
9

I waited until I finished my homework before I called Shoshanna back. She was in, and she needed a favor.

"Gideon and I were asked to play for a gathering that the president of the university is having, and I want to wear that silk suit of mine. Trouble is, I forgot to bring the shoes I always wear with it."

"The black ones with the straps?"

"Exactly. I think they're in the closet."

I walked over to the closet door and pried it open. No matter how many times my father fixes it, it always sticks. "They're here," I said.

"I don't have time to come home tomorrow. I have classes all day. Do you think you could bring them over after school?"

"Sure," I said, without hesitation, hoping I'd get a chance to see Gideon while I was there.

"Great. Chava said she'd meet you at the main gate. You're a life saver."

"That's a bit of an exaggeration," I said.

Shoshanna started to hang up, but I was too curious not to fish around—just a little. "Shosh—did you talk to Mom when you called?"

"Did I talk to her?"

"Did you leave a message on the machine, or did you actually talk to her?"

"We talked."

"Did she tell you?"

"Noa, I have a lot of work to do."

"Okay. I guess I should let her tell you."

"You mean about Ari?"

I was totally blown away. She said it just like that. Like Ari had decided to go to Elat for his spring vacation instead of coming home.

"I'm worried about him," I said.

"He'll be fine," she said, and I could hear that she just wanted to get off the phone.

Nine

"He's in jail," I reminded her.

"He's in a military prison, not jail, and it's safer there than in Hebron."

"I don't think that's why he went, Shoshanna."

"Regardless, it was a smart move."

"I'll meet Chava at the gate," I said, irritated. I hung up feeling as though I'd been dealt a double whammy. No one was acting like I had expected, except Ari himself.

I grabbed the stupid black shoes with the straps and threw them into my book bag.

CHAPTER
10

Okay, so I shouldn't have leaned over and kissed Matti on the cheek. I hadn't really meant anything by it. But the next day he kept looking over at me and smiling. I mean, what was I supposed to do? I had to smile back at him. I'm not a snob. I didn't want to hurt his feelings. But I also didn't want him to get any ideas, either. He tried to eat lunch with me, but luckily I was surrounded by my usual group of girlfriends. Minus one. She ate lunch with Aviva and some of the other girls. I stole a glance at her once or twice, but she refused to look at me.

I wondered if she'd wonder where I was going after school since I wouldn't be taking the bus home. I knew Matti would wonder.

I got off the bus near the security gate that surrounds the dormitories. Students were rushing out, headed across the road to the campus. I looked around.
Chava was chatting away with Tamar as a cute security guard checked someone's backpack, then waved her in.

"Hey," I said to Chava, as I dug Shoshanna's shoes out of my book bag and handed them to her.

"Hey, Noa. Tamar and I were just going over to Rachel's for coffee. Want to come along?"

We walked down the road and crossed the street, heading for Rachel's, a cafeteria complex that's run by the university. When we got to the guard station, Chava flashed her student ID and said I was with her.

The main cafeteria is huge and intimidating, so I was glad that Chava and Tamar wandered over to the crowded coffee bar. We ordered our coffees and walked toward eight students who were crowded around a table for four. They seemed relaxed, except for one girl whose eyes kept darting around the room.

"This is Noa," Chava said.

"Hey," a few of the students responded.

"Didn't we meet last weekend?" I asked one of the guys.

He looked over at me. "I don't think so," he said.

I moved aside the newspaper in front of me and put my cup down. "I thought you were a friend of my sister's."

"Who's your sister?"

"Shoshanna Bar Am."

"Don't know her," he said.

"The violinist," Chava said.

"Oh yeah," the girl with the darting eyes said. "You don't look anything like her."

"I know."

"Shoshanna doesn't even look Jewish."

"Michal," the guy said. "That's ridiculous."

"Yeah, I guess," Michal said, sounding unconvinced. She inhaled her cigarette, exhaled a stream of smoke, then butt the cigarette out in the already overflowing ashtray.

Michal really irritated me. So I leaned over and said, "Yeah, lots of people think my sister's the beautiful, talented one, but I'm the smart one."

"Smart enough," Tamar said, laughing.

I didn't really have trouble making friends of any age. Though, at that point, I seemed to have trouble keeping them.

I was feeling a little out of my element, and quite frankly, a little lonely as I walked to the bus stop, which was packed with people. Most of them were waiting for the bus to pull up before pushing and shoving their way onto it, but there was also a rudimentary line. I scanned the crowd. Who'd let me cut in? I didn't see anyone I knew. I'd have to talk someone into making room for me.

I was about to approach a tough-looking girl wearing a black leather jacket. She didn't look as if she gave a hoot about rules. Then I overheard two female students talking in loud, nervous voices about a suicide bomber. "Where?" I asked.

"In Tel Aviv," one of the students answered. "At a bus stop."

"It's a rumor," a student standing in front of her said. "It wasn't on the news."

"It's not a rumor," a woman insisted. "You'll see."

"I heard there was a *potential* suicide bombing," another guy said. "The bomb didn't go off."

I started getting nervous and thought about calling my mother and asking her to pick me up. But I didn't want her to know how I felt. She already had enough on her mind.

Then I noticed the Arab girl. I started walking over to her, but just as I was about to give her a big "remember me" smile, she turned away. This pissed me off. I had helped her. The least she could do was let me get in line in front of her.

"Hi," I said. I wasn't about to let her off the hook so easily. She turned her head slightly. We looked at each other, but we didn't speak. I could feel a certain tension, and suddenly cutting in line didn't seem all that important anymore, so I continued walking.

"Hey, Shoshanna's sister," I heard a moment later. I looked back at the Arab girl. She moved her head slightly, indicating that I could cut in front of her. I walked back. Neither of us said another word.

As soon as the bus pulled up, people started pushing and shoving. I admit it. I did a little pushing myself. But I wasn't aggressive enough to get a seat, and I found myself standing next to an Arab guy about my age. He didn't look at me, and I avoided looking at him. But I glanced over at the Arab girl, who was standing nearby, and I was suddenly embarrassed. Neither Shoshanna nor I had even bothered to ask her her name, so we just called her "the Arab girl" when we talked about her.

When the bus jerked to a stop a few minutes later, the Arab guy fell against me for a moment. Then he grabbed the pole more tightly. And I noticed that he'd broken out into a sweat.

The bus started up again, and I studied the guy carefully, glad I could hide my curiosity behind my sunglasses.

Why was he wearing a loose jacket? It was warm both outside and on the bus. Maybe he was sweating because he was wearing the jacket. Or maybe he was wearing the jacket because he was hiding something.

I looked around to see if anyone else was feeling as panicked as I felt. A few other passengers were also staring at the Arab guy, but mostly people were reading the newspaper or talking.

I concentrated on the area around the guy's waist and tried to determine whether or not he could be hiding something under his jacket. At this point, I'd broken out into a sweat myself. I could feel beads of perspiration on my forehead and under my armpits. Someone needs to check him out, I thought, just as he reached into his pocket and pulled out a cell phone.

At that moment, I lost all contact with my brain. In my imagination, I saw a horrifying image of that suicide bomber in Tel Aviv, the one who'd pulled out his cell phone and detonated a bomb he'd placed under some innocent girl's seat in another Egged bus.

"Suicide bomber," someone yelled. It took me a moment to realize that someone was me.

"Where? Where?" everyone screamed.

The driver stopped the bus. "Exit slowly—one by one," he said, calmly. But I could tell that he was looking at the Arab guy, too.

The Arab guy walked out ahead of me. He was very nervous, even more nervous than the rest of us. The driver said something to him, and he stepped to the side, his hands in the air, as the driver relieved him of his cell phone.

By the time I stepped off the bus, one policeman was questioning him while another was carefully inspecting the cell phone. All the passengers waited nearby and watched. The Arab girl looked at me angrily.

"No ID?" one policeman asked the Arab guy. The Arab guy shrugged.

"No bomb," the other policeman said. "Cell phone's just a cell phone."

I thought I saw the Arab girl smirk, but it may have been my imagination.

"No bomb, no ID, and no jobs in the occupied territories, either," the Arab girl said, looking directly at me.

When the police were satisfied that the Arab guy wasn't hiding anything, one of them asked who had yelled "suicide bomber." Several people stared at me as if I had single-handedly waged war against their peace of mind.

"I—I mean—I—"

"Is that the guy you thought was the suicide bomber?" one of the policemen asked.

I swallowed hard and nodded.

"Okay everybody, you can get back on the bus." The policeman looked at the Arab guy and nodded his head, indicating that he could get back on the bus, too, even though he had crossed the Green Line without the proper ID.

Everyone started pushing and shoving again, relieved that a catastrophe had been averted, although, of course, it had never been a real catastrophe, just one I had created in my overactive imagination. The policeman had said that it was better to be safe than sorry, but I was too embarrassed to reboard the bus. As I watched it pull away, I saw the Arab girl standing on the street corner, as well.

"We're not all terrorists," she said, bitterly.

"Obviously," I answered, a bit defensively. I wanted to tell her that she wasn't the first Muslim I'd ever talked to, that my parents and I had even gone to Nazareth to stay with Abed's family overnight. But I didn't think that would make much of an impact given the fact that I'd single-handedly caused a minor commotion, embarrassing myself and a poor kid with dirty fingernails who was probably trying to get home from some menial job that no Israeli wanted to do.

"I walk down the street in West Jerusalem, and all the Israelis glance at my book bag like I'm about to blow them up at any minute."

"Not everyone," I said, indignantly.

"You don't know what it's like. You have no idea what it's like to be the stranger in your own land."

I was going to stop her right there, tell her it wasn't her land anymore; it was ours. But it didn't seem like the right time to do that.

We started walking, though I don't think either of us had any idea where we were heading.

"I know you told Shoshanna and me where you live, but I can't remember."

"Abu Dis," she said, nodding in the direction of the Old City. "In the occupied territory annexed to Jerusalem," she added, emphasizing "occupied" and "annexed" as if to point out that annexation wasn't exactly a choice. Which, of course, it wasn't. But as far as I was concerned, she was lucky to be living in the Israeli half—which I assumed because she was enrolled at Hebrew University. She could travel all over Israel without restrictions. But obviously as far as she was concerned, she was living under an occupier's thumb as a second-class citizen.

"I suppose you know Israeli settlers living in the hills surrounding us," she said, sarcastically.

"I've never even been in the occupied territories!" I was close to shouting at her now.

"Really? You've never been to the Old City?"

"That's not the same thing. We captured the Old City in '67, but—"

She stopped walking and stared at me. "Exactly."

"But there aren't really settlers in the Old City—just the shops and the holy places, and—"

"Yeah, and—"

"But it's not like the settlements."

"How come you've never been to any of them—the settlements on the West Bank?"

"Because I don't know anyone who lives there. It's like a different world. I mean, they're settlers. They're not like real Israelis. Most of them are religious fanatics! Americans! I mean, yeah, there are Israelis too, but—"

The girl started to laugh.

"What?"

"They sure have a lot of power—for not being 'real' Israelis."

"Yeah, well, there are Arabs in the government, too."

The girl laughed again.

I knew why she was laughing, but it bugged me anyway. So the one or two Arabs in our parliament don't have all that much power, but there are plenty of Jews in Israel who speak up for Palestinians. How many Palestinians are there who speak up for Jews?

"How did you get into Hebrew University, anyway?" I asked, suddenly curious. It wasn't as if the place had a huge Arab population. In fact, I don't think there could have been more than a few Palestinian students there at the time.

"I'm smart," she answered.

"Are you Christian or Muslim?"

"You taking a survey?"

"Just curious."

"Muslim. I don't have to ask if you're a Jew."

"Well, I'm not one of those crazy religious Jews."

"I know. You're wearing shorts, aren't you?" She eyed my hair. "That's not a wig, is it? You've not covered from the neck down with some loose-fitting, ugly dress, are you?"

I started to laugh. "And you're not walking around in a *chador* and an *abaya*, covered from head to toe, looking like the last mourner on earth. So I guess you're not all that religious, either."

"We're not all—"

"I know. I know. You're not all fundamentalists."

Suddenly, we were both laughing, as if we'd known each other for years.

"I have to catch a bus," she said, and she turned to leave, still chuckling.

"Wait," I said, running after her. "I don't know your name."

"Maha," she called to the wind as she hurried off.

CHAPTER
11

I finally got home, promising myself that I wouldn't tell my parents about my outburst on the bus, but my mother was annoyed by my getting home so late, so I more or less had to tell her why. I also mentioned the Arab girl—Maha—in passing, and after I told her about that, I had to tell her about the first time we met in Shoshanna's room.

So my parents weren't that pleased about the incident in the room, but they didn't seem all that concerned about my taking a little walk with Maha, whose name my mother told me meant young gazelle. I remembered her leaping down the street, and I thought that fit her. Still, I couldn't concentrate on my homework that night. I wasn't exactly horrified by what I'd done on the bus, but I wasn't exactly happy about it, either. I wondered how guilty I'd look if people just assumed I was doing something wrong even when I wasn't.

Maybe that Arab kid had a right to be angry, even though he couldn't show it. Maybe Maha had a right to be angry.

While my conscience refused to let me off the hook, I was also excited by the sense of danger that preceded my embarrassment. I automatically reached for the phone to call Sarah. This was the kind of story I couldn't keep to myself, and I could just imagine Sarah screaming on the other end of the line as I dramatized the scenario on the bus, letting her believe—until the last minute—that the Arab guy might really have had a bomb.

Then I stopped myself. I couldn't call Sarah.

I suddenly felt very alone and completely disconnected. Sarah was the one person in my life who carried my secrets, things I could never share with anyone else. Losing her friendship meant that a deep part of me was cut off, and I had no other friend to affirm it.

I sunk down into my bed. Everyone liked Sarah. She was the sensitive one, the one who cared about everybody. Maybe I had lost more than a best friend.

Then I thought about Maha. She could be a friend. She was a friend. We'd laughed together. Doesn't that make people friends—if they can laugh together?

Maybe and maybe not, I decided. She hadn't asked me my name. And who could blame her? Shoshanna and I had tried to toss her out of the dorm, and I had just proved to her what a racist I was. She couldn't possibly like me.

CHAPTER
12

M r. Drucker, my chemistry teacher, looked surprised when I didn't turn in my homework. I couldn't tell him that I'd fallen asleep trying to decide how to keep myself from cringing inside when I saw an unfamiliar Arab walking toward me. I didn't want to be the kind of person who automatically thought that an Arab, any Arab, might be a suicide bomber, but if I were honest with myself I would have to admit that there were lots of times when I crossed the street to avoid passing an Arab. Was I just being cautious? Or was I prejudiced? One thing was for sure, by morning I was a wreck, but I knew that was no excuse for not doing my homework. I sneaked a look at Sarah, and she looked pretty surprised, too. But she didn't say a word. Part of me wished something really had happened on the bus. Then Sarah absolutely would have talked to me.

"Something the matter with you?" Matti asked.

"I'm okay."

"You don't look so good."

"Thanks."

"I mean, you look sick or something."

"I feel sick."

"Don't breathe on me. There's this lethal flu going around."

I looked at him with disgust. "I wouldn't think of breathing on you."

"You should have stayed home from school."

"You my doctor now?"

"No, it was just a suggestion."

"A stupid suggestion since I've already been at school all day, and this is last period."

"You don't have to be so bitchy about it. I was just trying to be nice."

"Well, don't try so hard."

"I won't," he said. And he moved away from me and started working on our lab experiment.

That's two down, I thought. Pretty soon everyone I know will be mad at me.

At the end of the period, Matti hurried out as I slowly gathered up my books and stuff. Not meaning to, I heaved a big sigh. Mr. Drucker looked up and cocked his head to the side.

"You feeling okay?" he asked.

"Not really."

"This is the first time you haven't turned in your homework."

"I know."

I heard Sarah and Aviva giggling as they walked off together.

"Think you'll be able to get it in tomorrow?"

"I don't know," I said, shrugging my shoulders.

Mr. Drucker got up from his desk and walked over to me.

"I don't know what's going on with you, and to tell you the truth, I don't much care, but I do care about your work. I've seen good students slide. A missed homework here and there, then a low grade on a quiz, and before you know it, they've gone from getting all 1s to getting all 3s."

"I get the point," I said, irritated.

"No, I don't think you do," he said.

"Okay, so maybe I don't." The words were out of my mouth before I could stop them. I had a moment of complete panic. Mr. Drucker did not accept this kind of talk from anyone. Mr. Drucker wasn't even the kind of teacher you could joke around with.

"Sit down, Noa," he said, firmly.

I could have appealed to his sympathy. I could have told him I was sick to my stomach the night before, but I decided not to. I decided that would, somehow, be cheating, even though it was true. I had been sick to my stomach and even sicker in my heart.

"Teenagers ride on emotional roller coasters. One minute you're up, and the next minute you're down. This is a proven fact. It's hormonal."

Yeah, I thought. What does that have to do with me?

"If you let yourself wallow in whatever it is that's bothering you, you'll be very sorry at the end of the semester when you look at your grade. You have a choice, Noa. You're a bright girl. You can choose to give in to your emotions, or you can choose to tell yourself that whatever it is that's bothering you will pass. Then you can get yourself together, stop staring into space, and start working again."

"You're right," I said, and I half meant it. I thought I might be sorry at the end of the semester, but, at the same time, I was thinking he was making a huge fuss over nothing. One missed homework assignment was no big deal. However, I hadn't done any of my other assignments either, and I didn't feel much like doing them that night.

I looked at Mr. Drucker and wondered how he knew that. "I am right," he said, and he walked back to his desk and started grading the homework papers without saying another word.

I barely made it to the school bus back to Beit Zeit, which was good because it didn't give me time to think. Even though I knew that the Arab guy wasn't a suicide bomber, I still had a lingering feeling that I'd gotten away with something. And that the next time I wouldn't be so lucky.

As embarrassed as I am to admit this, I had a flash of fear as I walked toward the back. Then I panicked for a moment when I realized that none of the safe seats were vacant. Well, what I considered the safe seats. But the panic passed. I knew all these kids on the bus. And once again, I felt completely guilty for feeling what I had felt.

I fell into an aisle seat next to Shimon, this incredibly nosy kid in my math class. Then I slowly moved my feet under the seat, checking to see if there might be a parcel there, which was totally ridiculous. But I did it anyway.

I automatically took out my cell phone and punched in my father's number.

"I'm on my way home," I said.

I was about to return the phone to my backpack when it rang. It was Shoshanna's number. My heart sank. I didn't want to answer it.

"Phone's ringing," Shimon said.

"Hi, Shosh."

"Thanks for dropping off the shoes."

"That's okay."

"Mom told me what happened."

I glanced over at Shimon, who seemed more interested in my conversation than I wanted him to be. "It was no big deal."

"Look, everybody's nervous these days. You—"

"He was just some poor kid trying to earn a few *shekels*," I said so loudly the kids sitting near me turned around to stare.

"Yeah, I know," Shoshanna said. Then I heard her sigh.

I hovered close to the window and whispered into the phone. "You think I overreacted, right?"

Shoshanna didn't say anything for a moment. Then she said quietly, "I talked to Mom right before the concert, so I didn't really have a chance to give it much thought."

"Concert a success?" I asked, feeling more than a little relieved.

"It was great."

"Say hi to Gideon for me."

She chuckled. "Oh, I almost forgot. Rebekah said that Arab girl asked for your phone number."

"My phone number? She's going to call me?"

"What is *that* about?"

CHAPTER
13

" She's a friend of Shoshanna's roommate?" my mother asked for the third time.

"Sort of," I answered for the third time. "I told you—I met her when she spent the night in Shoshanna's room."

"But she's in college. What could she want with you?"

"She's only a year or two older than me. She didn't exactly have to go into the army before college," I countered. "Anyway, we got into sort of a political discussion, and—"

"It's very nice of her family to invite you to their home," my father said, coming to my defense.

"But Abu Dis," my mother countered.

"She lives on the Israeli side. Not the Palestinian side. And it's not like she lives in a refugee camp. Besides, it's probably safer than Ben Yehudah Street," I said boldly, pretending that my stomach wasn't being attacked by a flutter of butterflies. I had accepted Maha's invitation without stopping to think about what I would feel like actually going to Abu Dis. It had sounded really exciting. And I was curious about her, about her family, about a place I'd never seen, even though it had been part of Jerusalem since 1967. "Why would bombs go off *there*?" I added, more to reassure myself than my mother.

As we drove past the Old City, south of the Mount of Olives toward Abu Dis, I wished that Maha hadn't asked us to meet her at the barrier separating the Israeli half of the city from the Palestinian half. Barriers make me feel queasy. Living in Beit Zeit, we don't have to actually see them, just read about them, hear about them, and talk about them. But Maha had said it would be easier to meet at the checkpoint than to find her house. Still, as we approached the barrier, my excitement catapulted into anxiety. What if something happened? What if the IDF suddenly marched into town, and I got caught in the middle of the turmoil?

"Why can't we drive you there—to her house?" my mother asked.

"I don't know where she lives. You can give her the third degree when you meet her," I said, laughing at my mother's nervousness. Secretly, I wished my parents had been invited, as well. I knew, given the tensions, that it wasn't possible for them to take a tour of Abu Dis while I was hanging out with Maha, but I also knew they were going shopping in downtown Jerusalem, only fifteen minutes away. They had their cell phones. I had my cell phone, I told myself. Abu Dis was still Israel, even if there weren't any Jews living there.

I stared at the series of movable, squat cement blocks that formed barriers at the checkpoint adjacent to a small, open, makeshift building. That was before the Israeli government built the concrete wall three meters high that divides Abu Dis right down the middle, making it even more impossible to go from the Palestinian section still supervised by the Israeli government to the Palestinian section supervised by the Palestinians. Though Arabs with the proper ID are allowed to travel all over Israel, Palestinians who live on the other side of the barrier have a really hard time crossing the line because the road is often closed for security reasons. And Jews aren't even allowed into the Palestinian-run part of Abu Dis. Though the road was open that day, there seemed to be an incredibly long wait for Palestinians to get from the Palestinian side to the Israeli side—that is, for those Palestinians actually lucky enough to get special permits to cross the checkpoint into Israel. I guess they had such a long wait because their cars were often stopped and searched. To tell you the truth, I had very mixed feelings about that. On the one hand, I was glad their cars were being searched because that made it more difficult for terrorists to get through. On the other hand, I was embarrassed to be a witness to the humiliation of ordinary people who just happened to have been born outside of the Jerusalem city line.

Out of the backseat car window, I spotted Maha.

"There she is," I said, pointing to a girl standing at the checkpoint, arguing with one of the soldiers.

My father stopped the car and leaped out. I followed. My mother got behind the wheel and moved the car to the side of the road.

The soldier, who looked young and mean, pushed Maha, screaming at her to get away from the border.

"I live here. You can't make me move. I have to meet someone. You've already searched me. No bombs. No nothing. You checked my ID twice. What do you want?"

My father and I were running now.

"You can't wait here." He gave her a shove. Even from a distance, I could see the anger in Maha's face and knew that she wanted to shove him back, but if she so much as shifted in that direction, she would be arrested.

"Go ahead, beat me up," she seethed, "but I'm not moving."

The soldier raised his fist as if that were exactly what he was going to do, but my father planted himself in front of him, and the soldier dropped his arm. "She's waiting for us," my father said, respectfully. I'm sorry if we've caused you any inconvenience."

"Papers," the soldier demanded.

My father reached into his pocket and took out his ID, but I was sure the soldier knew my father was an Israeli Jew before he even looked at it.

I handed him my ID, as well. The soldier looked at my father and shook his head. "It's dangerous for Jews to be here," he said, angrily. "What's wrong with you people?"

"We'll meet you back here at four o'clock," my father said, ignoring the soldier and smiling at me and Maha as we moved away from the checkpoint. He extended his hand to Maha. "I'm David, Noa's father."

"I'm Maha," she said, without taking his hand. She was trying to dampen the anger she couldn't quite contain and couldn't really express.

As we walked through the streets of Abu Dis, I noticed a group of people wearing black and white *kuffias* that billowed from thin, black, rope-like headbands. They were staring at us. They know I'm Jewish, I kept thinking. They hate me. My head felt heavy, as if it were the receptacle for dozens of unspoken insults. I lowered it and stared at the ground. I wanted to walk closer to Maha for protection, but she kept me at a distance. We hadn't exchanged a word since we left the checkpoint. Maybe coming here was a mistake, I thought. Maybe we were both sorry I was there.

We walked through the town, and, unexpectedly, it seemed almost indistinguishable from downtown West Jerusalem. Though there weren't any Gap or Apple stores like there were in West Jerusalem, there were grocery stores, furniture stores, clothing stores, and little cafés and restaurants. There were parking lots, a post office, apartment buildings. I was pretty surprised and impressed. It looked like any other Israeli suburb, though the public areas could have used a good cleaning and revitalization crew. But there was one really big difference: posters with pictures of suicide bombers were plastered on several walls and a banner with a picture of Arafat stretched over the street. Reason enough for the IDF to march in and tear them down. Maha didn't seem to notice them, but they literally made me sick. I broke into a sweat and felt like throwing up.

Instead, I took a deep breath, hoping I didn't look as bad as I felt, and I followed Maha down a wide street with modern, expensive villas—much nicer than my house. I began to feel a little better; no terrorists stared down at me from those walls.

Finally, we veered off to a side street that suddenly opened up to a small compound of very old but well-kept limestone houses with arched doorways. We passed a few kids aiming their sling shots at some tin cans. They didn't bother looking up when we walked past, which was a relief.

Maha strode up a stone path into a little courtyard. Red and purple bougainvillea exploded on both sides of the path, and oranges drooped from trees. She nodded to me, and we entered a house that reminded me of Gideon's—until we walked into the living room. The first thing I noticed was a miniature Dome of the Rock displayed on a side table. A large hand-woven rug lay in the middle of the floor, and several uncomfortable looking couches surrounded it. Lots of chairs were pushed up against the walls as if to prevent the walls from tumbling down—or being torn down. The only other furniture in the room was a low, round, brass-topped table with large red and gold silk cushions scattered on the floor around it and several floor to ceiling bookcases. Though it didn't make any rational sense, I felt more at ease once I noticed the bookcases.

Maha and I still hadn't spoken. I was starting to wonder if I should say something when an elegant-looking woman walked into the room carrying a tray with a pitcher of juice and juice glasses. Her long black hair was slicked back into a bun, and she was wearing the kind of dress my mother might have worn if she had better taste.

"You must be hot," she said to me.

"Yes, I am."

"Maha, please introduce me to your friend so I can thank her for allowing you to spend the night in her dorm room."

"This is Noa. Noa, this is my mother, Mona Hijazi, and she's not the one who allowed me to stay in her room; it was her sister."

Mrs. Hijazi studied Maha's face for a moment. "What happened?" she asked quietly.

I braced myself, expecting Maha to go into a tirade, condemning the soldier at the checkpoint to everlasting damnation, but to my surprise she just reached for the pitcher and poured herself a glass of juice. "The heat made me sick," she said.

"It was my sister's decision," I said, "but I was glad she let Maha stay." I didn't add that I had been terrified the whole night, wondering if she'd hidden a bomb in the closet.

Mrs. Hijaz smiled at me. "Please make yourself comfortable, Noa. Lunch will be ready soon."

I watched her as she swept across the room to what I assumed was the kitchen. "Your mother's nice," I said. Then I started to laugh, mostly out of nervousness. "Nice? What's that supposed to mean? I hate that word. Nice is boring. Harmless but boring."

"My mother's not nice," Maha said. "She's strong and smart, but she's not necessarily nice."

"Oh," I said, and I stopped laughing.

"She's nice maybe in the way you mean—nice to strangers, nice to her family and friends, but she's not nice. She's angry."

"Yeah," I said. "I guess I can't blame her."

Maha looked at me hard. I couldn't tell what she was thinking, and it made me uncomfortable.

"Really? And why is that?" she asked, sarcastically.

"Well, I—I mean—"

"Who do you blame then?"

"Well, I just mean, I, you know, I can understand why she might be angry."

"No, you can't."

"Well, maybe not exactly, but—"

"Not at all."

"Maybe 'understand' is the wrong word."

"You have no idea what my mother has gone through. What it's like for us."

"I'm not stupid."

"But you're naïve."

"Okay. Maybe I am. But I do know that it can't be easy for you to—to have to argue with an Israeli soldier in order to stand on the street in your own city."

"You got that right."

"Maha, I'm really sorry. It must have been incredibly hum—"

"You're not sorry," she spat out.

I was shocked and confused. Somehow everything had gotten totally turned around, and I had become the enemy—because what Maha had said was partially true.

"You're not sorry because you're glad it was me being verbally attacked by an Israeli soldier and not you being attacked by a Palestinian soldier. My family has lived here—in Abu Dis—for five generations. My grandfather was the mayor. How do you think he would feel if he saw that some stranger had the power to decide where I could and could not walk in my own city? Your people took everything from us—our land, our history, our ancient olive trees. The very sky above our heads is pierced by Israeli helicopters invading our space."

"Maha," her mother said, sternly, as she suddenly appeared in the doorway carrying a tray of salads. "Noa is a guest in our house."

"We used to visit our cousins in Nablus," Maha continued, as if she hadn't heard the tone of her mother's voice. "Now it's easier to drive to Jordan—another country—than it is to get through all the checkpoints."

"That is not Noa's fault," her mother said. "I don't know what's troubling you today. Please, Noa, sit down, and we can have our lunch."

As I slowly moved toward the silk cushions on the floor, I noticed a group of photographs on the mantle above the fireplace. Hoping to change the subject and ease the tension, I nodded toward a posed photograph of Maha, her mother, a man, and a teenaged boy, and asked, "Your family?"

Maha nodded, but I could still feel her tension. There was another photo of the boy, a large photo elaborately framed. I moved closer to it. The boy was very handsome. Then I spotted a familiar face in a group photograph of smiling people waving at the camera. "That's Abed!"

"You know Abed?" Maha asked, surprised.

"He's one of my father's good friends. Actually, he's an old family friend," I said, hesitantly. I didn't know how Maha would respond.

"Abed is my cousin," Maha's mother said.

I smiled tentatively.

"We used to go to the beach in Herzliya with Abed," Maha said, wistfully, as if the mention of his name was a salve for her pain.

"I've known him forever. He and my dad ride horseback together, and—" I was almost afraid to say it. "And they belong to an Israeli/Palestinian dialogue group."

"Perhaps some day we'll all be able to speak to one another," Maha's mother said, as she poured juice into my glass. "Then all the shooting will end, and the prison gates will open, and innocent boys will come home to their families."

Yes, I thought, innocent boys like my brother. I was going to tell them about Ari, but just then I noticed a look of sadness pass between Maha and her mother and realized it wasn't the right time. I was afraid it might feel as if I were bragging.

"I'm going to be a doctor," Maha said. "And work in the occupied territories with Abed."

"Maybe they won't be occupied by the time you finish university and medical school," I said, quietly.

Maha looked at me for a long moment, then the tension finally began to drain out of the room.

"Maybe not," she said.

We all started talking about Abed. I told them that he kept his horse in our backyard. Maha told me that he had helped her get into the Hebrew University because of his connections. We laughed about what we call *protectzia*, knowing someone in the government who can help you get what you need. We talked about movies. We talked about chemistry and math. It was almost as if the nightmare part of the day had been tucked under one of the silk cushions and forgotten.

CHAPTER
14

My parents were waiting for me at the checkpoint. My mother's face, wary and worried, settled into relief when she spotted me. Gracious, as always, she invited Maha to our house, and we made arrangements to pick her up after Passover and drive her to Beit Zeit.

"We would like to invite your whole family," she added, but Maha smiled her ironic smile and said, without further explanation, that it wouldn't be possible.

My parents weren't surprised to learn that Abed was a distant cousin, given the fact that he had tons of relatives all over Israel and the territories. But I think just knowing about that link between Maha's family and ours formed a sort of trust between us. We speculated about why it wasn't possible for her family to visit Beit Zeit, and, in the end, we agreed that probably one of her parents was living in the Israeli section illegally and didn't have the proper ID.

Maha's father, who had come home after lunch, had told me he was a high school teacher, but her mother hadn't said anything about her work. Her father had talked about how frustrating his job had become because he couldn't get simple things like pencils and paper. Books apparently were more than scarce, so he brought his own books from home and read them out loud to his classes. Like Maha, he spoke Hebrew with barely an accent, and I was embarrassed because my Arabic consists of a few swear words and common terms like *habibi* and *yallah*, "my friend" and "let's go."

Maha's father also knew a lot about Israeli writers and poets, and once again I was at a loss. We never studied Arabic writers in our schools, though the Arabs living in Israel proper were forced to teach the work of Israeli writers in theirs.

I had kept hoping Maha's brother would come home so I could meet him, but he hadn't. I admit I never quite lost my nervous feeling about being with an Arab family I didn't really know, but toward the end of the afternoon, I sort of forgot how different we were and began to focus on our similarities. When Maha was with her parents that edginess that emanated from her like porcupine needles receded. And her ironic sense of humor made me laugh, rather than cringe. I stopped feeling guilty because I had been born a Jewish Israeli with the proper ID.

Fourteen

Still, I sensed that a sort of sadness had draped itself over the house. I couldn't explain why, but it felt like the sadness that had seeped into our house since Ari had been in prison. But classical music filled Maha's house, too, and some of the same books lined the shelves in the living room. We ate the same Middle Eastern food I had eaten at Gideon's house, the same food my mother picked up at the market. During lunch, I had glanced at the picture of her brother again. In another world, he and Ari could pass for brothers.

CHAPTER
15

The whir of the table saw sliced the air as I opened the door. My father didn't hear me come in, so I stood there looking at him for a moment. I could see what people meant when they said I look like him, though he's not that tall for a man, and I'm pretty tall for a girl.

We have very different personalities though. My father is the one who, in his quiet way, tries to appease everyone, to make everyone happy. And I, in my not so quiet way, am often the one who causes the problem in the first place.

As if feeling my presence, my father looked up. Then he finished the cut he was making and turned off the saw. He wiped his hands on his jeans and walked through the sawdust covering the floor.

"What are you making?"

"A cabinet for the Aboulafias."

"It's nice."

"I think so."

"Did you make the call?"

"I did."

"You don't look very happy. I guess that means we can't go tomorrow," I said. I knew that my voice was quivering, and I didn't want to say anything else.

My father shook his head. "They won't let us see him yet."

"What about the day after?"

"No visits yet. Only from his lawyer. Those are the rules."

"Will we be able to see him before Passover?"

"I don't think so."

"What will we do?"

"We'll pick up Mimi as planned, and go to Vered ha-Galil over night. Then come back to Netanya for the seder."

"I don't want to go. It'll be horrible without Ari. Ari loves Vered ha-Galil."

"Mimi's expecting us."

"I know," I said, sadly.

Totally disappointed about not being able to see Ari, I headed back to the house to sulk. "Why does this Passover have to be different from all other Passovers?" I muttered to myself. It was bad enough that Ari was in prison. But two weeks ago Mimi decided that we should all go up to Vered ha-Galil, a dude ranch, and spend a few days together before Passover. When my mother protested, saying we wouldn't have time to prepare for the seder, Mimi said she'd already taken care of that. She'd made reservations for us to have seder at a hotel.

Mom was a little upset because she liked the ritual of the three of us cooking together. The three of us because Shoshanna hated to cook. She wouldn't touch the gefilte fish because it smells so bad. And she was afraid her fingers would be contaminated, or something. And chopping anything was totally out of the question. What if the knife had slipped and injured her finger? So it was just Mom, Mimi, and me. It was a lot of work, but it was fun, a family tradition. Now we weren't even going to do that.

Mimi used to come to our house to cook, but after she moved to Netanya, we'd go there, which was great. Because her apartment was just across the street from the ocean, it was like a mini vacation.

Mimi had moved to Netanya because she thought it was safer than living in Jerusalem. But she said it was because there were so many French-speaking people in Netanya, and it made her feel young again.

Mimi grew up in Paris. But when she was fourteen, her parents sent her to live on the French Riviera. It was during World War II, and they thought it was safer there—for Jews. And it was safer—for most of the war. But then Mimi and many other Jews were rounded up and placed in transit camps. From there Mimi was herded onto the last French train headed for Auschwitz. She didn't like to talk about the train or about being in a concentration camp. She liked to talk about the people who helped her in Nice. She liked to talk about the sound of the ocean at night. She liked to talk about making footprints in the sand and thinking if the waves didn't wash them away by morning she'd survive another day.

From the balcony of her apartment in Netanya, Mimi could see the Mediterranean coast and dream about the Riviera. She liked to watch Israeli soldiers patrolling the coast. And she loved the "handsome young policemen" who inspect purses and bags before anyone can enter a store or a movie theater, the symphony, or a mall, even some pizza parlors.

"Jewish soldiers," she always said. "If only we'd had Jewish soldiers in France."

Mimi was someone to be reckoned with. She was the matriarch of the family, and her decision was like the word of God. Not even my mother argued with her.

I wandered into the kitchen and opened the refrigerator, hoping to find some consolation. Cottage cheese, olives, carrots, yogurt—they wouldn't do it. I grabbed a jar of peanut butter and a spoon. There was no time to spread it on bread. I needed instant gratification. After two spoons full, I gave up and reached for a glass of water, glad that I couldn't find any cookies because I would eat the whole box given the way I was feeling.

I walked into my bedroom and picked up my cell phone. I could call my sister, but she wasn't the kind of sister who encouraged heart-to-hearts. I wanted to call Ari, but that wasn't possible. And, of course, I couldn't call Sarah, either, though she was the person I really wanted to talk to. I scrolled down my list of contacts and stopped at Maha's name.

"Hey," I said when she answered her cell.

"Hey, Noa, I was just thinking about you."

"Really?" I asked, gratified because she reinforced the connection I hoped we had made.

"Yeah, I heard that Madonna's giving a concert and wondered if you wanted to go. I can get tickets at school."

"Madonna? As in *the* Madonna?"

"As in *the* Madonna. She's supposedly studying Kabbalah and is coming to Israel to spread her newly discovered Jewish mysticism around."

"Very funny."

"No, I'm serious. I read an article about it."

"That's a riot. I can't wait to tell Ari."

"Who's Ari?"

I held my breath for a moment. "My—ah—brother."

"Wow, you don't seem so sure about that. What did he do, rob a bank, or something, and get disowned by your family?"

"Not exactly, although you're sort of right about one thing. He is in prison."

I heard Maha take a deep breath and hold it for a long time before she let it escape.

"Ari's in the army."

I could hear her breathing kind of rapidly now, but she didn't say anything.

"Are you there?"

"Yes," she said, but she suddenly sounded as if she were a hundred miles away.

"I was going to tell you about him the other day."

"Is he in the army, or is he in prison?" she asked, her voice cracking, as if we had a bad connection.

"Both."

"Why do I feel like we're going around in circles here?"

"Sorry. I get a little jumpy when I talk about Ari. I'm never sure how people are going to react."

"So, what's the deal?"

"He is in the army, but he refused to serve in the occupied territories, so he is in a military prison," I said, quickly, hoping to get it out before she could hear the trembling in my voice.

"I wish you had told me that before."

"Why?"

"I wouldn't have been so hard on you."

"Yes, you would have. I acted like a crazy person that day on the bus."

"You're right; you did."

"Well, you don't have to agree with me."

"Yes, I do," she said, and she started to laugh.

That's what I liked about Maha. She could be totally serious and totally upset, but she could also snap out of it and see humor in the most serious situations.

"So I suppose you like me better now," I said.

"Not really. You're not in prison; your brother is."

"Don't I get any points for that?"

"Hey, give me a break. I liked you before you told me about your brother."

And that did it. I had gotten exactly what I needed. If my mother had walked in and handed me a box of cookies at that moment, I would have told her I wasn't hungry any more.

CHAPTER

16

The day before we left for Netanya, my mother gave me an assignment. She'd been so busy with school that she hadn't had a chance to choose a gift for Mimi as a thank you for our trip to Vered ha-Galil. "Pick something wonderful," she had said.

"I don't know what her taste is."

"Yes, you do. It's the opposite of yours."

I was about to grouse about it, but decided to call Maha instead to see if she had time to go shopping.

We met in front of Hamashbir, a department store in the middle of town, and for a moment I was sorry that I had suggested meeting there. I hadn't given the guard a second thought until we stood in front of him. I knew that he would give my purse a cursory check and go through everything in hers.

But I was wrong. He let her pass after a brief check and went through everything in my bag.

When we got inside the store, we looked at each other and started to laugh. Yes, I thought, this is what friendship is all about. We trust each other enough to laugh about what just happened.

Maha suggested buying Mimi a scarf, but Mimi had a million scarves, so we just wandered around until we found ourselves in a department that just happened to carry the kind of clothes we both just happened to like—a lot.

We tried on some very cool t-shirts and the best-fitting jeans in the world. There was no way either of us could walk away empty-handed, so she took out her mother's credit card, and I took out my mother's credit card, and those jeans somehow wound up in our possession, though I knew my mother would kill me when I got home.

We walked the exit of the store, feeling as if we had won the lottery. Then Maha thrust her arm in front of me to stop me from walking one step farther.

"Forget something?"

I looked down at my department store bag to make sure I had those precious jeans.

"No."

"You sure?"

My mouth dropped open. "Oh yeah. I guess I got side-tracked."

"Perfume?"

"The last thing she needs."

"Jewelry?"

"She has a ton already."

"Cards?"

"What?"

"Does she play cards?"

"Poker. Why?"

Maha nodded toward an automatic card shuffler on a nearby counter.

"Perfect."

So, the next morning, as planned, we packed up the car, including Mimi's gift, perfectly wrapped; and my mom, my dad, Shoshanna, and I drove to Netanya to pick her up.

No one said anything for a long time. I guess we were all thinking about Ari and his not being with us. Then my dad reached over and turned on the car radio. "A gunman opened fire on Israeli soldiers in Hebron who were patrolling near the Tomb of the Patriarchs."

I stopped breathing. "One soldier was killed and five were wounded."

Shoshanna was right. Ari *was* better off in jail. He could have been one of those soldiers.

Yeah, I'm embarrassed to say that. But it's the truth. I was sorry those soldiers were hurt. I was very sorry one soldier died. But I can't deny I was relieved that none of those soldiers was Ari.

As if Mimi had read my mind, she opened the car door and said, "I just heard the news. Thank God Ari's not in Hebron. But it's too bad he couldn't get off duty in time to meet us at Vered ha-Galil."

No one responded, which meant my mother still hadn't told Mimi that Ari wouldn't be coming to seder, either.

Shoshanna and I squeezed over, so Mimi could slip into the back seat with us.

"The political situation is simply getting out of hand," Mimi said, as soon as we took off. "It's totally ruined the tourist business. Shops are closing. Hotels are empty. The whole country is going to go bankrupt if things aren't settled soon."

"That's true," my father said. "Maybe the government should hire you as a consultant, Mimi."

He didn't say this sarcastically. He meant it. My father thought Mimi had a great sense of business. Sometimes he'd shake his head and say, "Boy, if I could market myself like Mimi does, I'd be able to hire enough assistants to triple my output."

Mimi had actually invented a beauty product and owned a company that manufactures it. It's a cream for your skin made from avocados and other fruits and vegetables. I guess if you were starving, you could eat it.

After my grandfather went back to Germany, she needed to make a living for her and my mother. Her family had been in the cosmetics business in France, so this was a natural choice for her. She didn't expect the business to do so well, but I think you can buy the cream all over Europe and the United States now.

But Dad's a dreamer. I don't think he really ever wanted to triple his business. Then he wouldn't be able to work alone. He'd have to tell his assistants what to do all the time, and he'd hate that. And there's also the problem that he isn't able to criticize people. He can always see their perspective. "Live and let live," he says. "Their point of view is just as valid as mine."

My mother used to get furious with him. They had the same argument a dozen times. "There is right and wrong, David," she'd say. "A moral right and wrong."

He'd shake his head and smile. "I agree with you," he'd say, "but the hard part is to determine whose moral perspective is right and whose is wrong."

They never *really* agreed about some things, but they never seemed to get tired of going over the same arguments.

Me? I was caught in the middle. Like I said, I wish the world were more like math, but it's not. So, yeah, I think there's a right and wrong, but I also think sometimes you have to decide for yourself what that right and wrong should be. Like Ari. Or maybe like Sarah.

Nothing had ever been resolved between Sarah and me. We had just drifted away from each other. At least my parents talked about their disagreements, and even if I got sick of hearing their arguments, they were communicating—or, at least, trying to.

"Remind me to call Sarah when we get back," I said to no one in particular.

"How come she hasn't been around lately?" Mom asked. "Haven't you two made up yet?"

"Don't tell me Noa and Sarah had an argument," Shoshanna said. "They're practically glued together."

"She should really do something about that hair of hers," Mimi said.

"She likes her hair the way it is, Mimi," I said with a slight edge to my voice.

"It is kind of unflattering," Shoshanna said.

"Well, we all can't have silky, blond hair like yours," I snapped back at her.

"Aren't we a bit touchy?" she said.

"That's enough, girls," my mother said.

"More than enough," I said under my breath.

Okay, so I liked to get in the last word. It made me feel better.

CHAPTER
17

The sky was clear as we drove up the mountain, and the sun was still high enough for us to go horseback riding that afternoon. As soon as my father turned into the road to Vered ha-Galil, we all breathed more easily. Both the tensions in the car and the tensions we always live with suddenly began to fade away.

We continued driving up the mountain above the Sea of Galilee and eased into paradise. Vered ha-Galil—Rose of the Galilee—was the only resort Mimi actually loved. It's cosmopolitan, she would say. It could be anywhere in the world.

We divided up into two cabins. Each cabin had a living room, a bathroom, and two bedrooms. My parents and I were in one cabin, and Mimi and Shoshanna in the other. After glancing around, we slung our bags on the beds and walked out to the stable. Shoshanna came to see us off, but she was going to practice her violin while we rode up to the Mount of Beatitudes and back.

We mounted our horses, then lined up behind our guide from the ranch. The paths are steep and not always visible, so even though we'd ridden here before, the staff at the ranch insisted that a guide lead us. Mimi went first as we wound our way even farther up the mountain where wild flowers had popped up, coloring the mountainside with reds and yellows.

Spring was my favorite time of year. Even though remnants of sadness remained, the last rains of winter had washed away uninvited frustration. I wanted to celebrate Passover, as we did every year, welcoming nature's visual feast. Our seder table always had three centerpieces: the traditional seder plate, a plate containing the first vegetables of spring, and a huge vase with spring flowers. I didn't think the hotel would dare upstage the traditional seder plate by putting vegetables and flowers on the tables. And I would miss them.

We rode in silence, passing several Bedouin tents. Two short slender men with deeply lined faces sat in front of one tent playing *sheshbesh*, which the Americans call backgammon. I thought about Ari. He loves *sheshbesh*. I never had the patience to learn how to play.

In front of another tent, several Bedouin women retrieved laundry from a makeshift laundry line. Their heads were covered in dark scarves, and they were dressed in what looked like long, shapeless purple sacks tied at the waist. But running down the sides of the dresses were narrow, colorfully embroidered patterns. The same stitching was woven into a yoke covering their chests. The youngest woman, who was probably no older than I was, smiled at me as we rode past. Another woman waved, making creases in her leathery skin. When she opened her mouth to smile, I could see the gap where two of her front teeth had been. I was embarrassed for her, but she didn't seem to mind. She looked happier than me. I felt guilty enjoying the freedom and quiet of these hills while my brother was cooped up in a cell. I looked back at the Arab women, who'd returned to their work. They seemed to belong to another world in another century when life was simpler.

We reached the Mount of Beatitudes after an hour or so and dismounted. That was our destination for the day. We were all glad we hadn't decided to take one of the longer treks because we were already hot and tired, and the cold water from the fountain tasted clean and fresh. We talked softly, not because we'd disturb anyone, but because it felt right. The magical silence on the ledge hovered over us, almost like a blessing.

     I stretched my limbs and felt like purring. Then I walked around a little to shake out my body. I looked down on the Sea of Galilee, where Jesus supposedly walked on water. I was standing where he had preached his sermon on the mount. History is alive for us in Israel. We actually go to Masada, the Dead Sea, and the tombs of Rachael and Mary. We walk down the streets of Jerusalem, like the Via Dolorosa or King David Street. But there are other historical places we cannot go. Hebron and Bethlehem are now under the control of the Palestinian Authority and off-limits to Israelis unless they have special permission to enter.

     Generally, I take these places for granted. This country is my home. It always has been. I don't usually think about things that took place here thousands of years ago. But when I'm standing in some ancient biblical site like the Mount of Beatitudes, I seem to get flooded with memories that aren't even mine.

     While I was sitting quietly by myself, lost in the past, Mimi slipped over to me. She put her arm around me, not something she did very often, and whispered in my ear, "You going to tell me what's going on?"

     I looked at her, surprised.

     "What do you mean?"

     "Oh, I think you know what I mean," she said. "And you're the one person in the family who will give me a direct and honest answer."

"About what?" I asked, nervously. I knew about what, but I was stalling. I looked around for help, but my mother and father and the guide were walking down into the garden.

"Needless to say, I've known your mother all her life. And she is not very good at hiding things—which is perhaps why she was never interested in the cosmetics business," she added with a little smile. Mimi was sharp.

"Something's going on with Ari," she said.

"How'd you know?"

"A good businesswoman is also a good mind reader. There was too much tension in the air when his name came up. Now—are you going to tell me, so we can have a pleasant ride back, or do I have to wheedle it out of your mother?"

"I think you should wheedle it out of my mother."

"That will be such hard work, darling, and I do need some relaxation time. He got the wrong girl pregnant, I suppose, and everyone's trying to cover it up until he and the girl decide what to do. Poor Ari. I think we can count on him to do the right thing. Now you and I—we'd do the most practical thing, wouldn't we?"

I wasn't sure this was a compliment, although I was sure my grandmother thought it was. Sometimes I wished people thought I was as nice as sweet, sensitive Ari.

"He didn't get anyone pregnant. He's in jail."

Mimi started to laugh. She obviously didn't believe me.

"Sorry, Mimi, but it's true. Ari is in jail."

For a moment she just opened her eyes wide and stared at me. Then she straightened her back and pulled up her shoulders, preparing her defenses. I could feel the gates to her heart clang shut. And I shivered despite the heat.

"You had better start from the beginning," she said, calmly. Too calmly.

I didn't know what to say. I felt caught in my own trap.

"I'm waiting, Noa."

So I told her. She didn't say a word. So I started blathering on about Ari's doing the right thing, and about Mom and Dad thinking it was the right thing to do, too. "I'd refuse to serve in the territories," I said. "I'd do exactly what Ari's doing."

Mimi reached over and slapped me across the face. Then without a word, she walked across the marble floor of the patio, got on her horse, and started back down the mountain.

When the guide saw her, he yelled, "Stop, Giveret Krause, you cannot return without me. It's forbidden."

Mimi paid no attention. She just kept on riding.

My mother and father ran over to me. "What happened?" my mother cried. "Where's she going?"

I ran my hand over my cheek, which burned with pain and humiliation. I didn't trust myself to say anything.

My mother just stared at me, while the guide motioned for us to join him as he ran toward the horses.

"You should have let your mother tell Mimi," my father said.

My mother jerked her head around to look at him. Then she looked at me.

"Did you tell her about Ari?"

I nodded my head.

"Let's go," the guide yelled at us. He had already mounted his horse and was waiting.

"Noa, one of these days, you're going to get into a lot of trouble unless you learn to keep things to yourself," my mother said. Then she just shook her head and walked across the patio to her horse.

My father didn't say anything. But he put his arm around me, and we walked toward our horses together.

CHAPTER

18

The atmosphere at dinner was horrendous that evening. I was angry at Mimi. My mother was mad at me. And Mimi was furious with all of us. The minute we sat down at the table, she announced that I had told her Ari was in a military prison.

"Do you really think it's necessary to hide information about the family from me, Lilah?" she asked my mother.

"I was going to tell you in the morning," my mother said. "I just wanted us to enjoy this time together."

"How can you enjoy yourself when your son's in prison? When your son has chosen to go to prison, I might add."

"We're all worried about Ari," my father said. "We wish things were different, but—"

"So you don't agree with this crazy notion of his?"

"I do agree," my father said. "If I were called up to serve in the territories, I'd protest in the same way Ari's protesting."

I held my breath, wondering if Mimi would slap my father across the face, as well.

Instead she gave him her famous steely look, then turned to my mother.

"And you? What do you think?"

"We all agree, Mama."

"You're a very bad influence on your children," Mimi said to my mother and father. "I'm disappointed in both of you."

I wanted to rush to my parents' defense, but I was so angry at Mimi I was afraid of what I might say. So I just sat there, biting my bottom lip.

"This is a terrible time," my mother said, without looking directly at Mimi. I could see that she was trying very hard not to lose control of her emotions. "All of our hopes and dreams for our country are being turned upside down. Everyone's living under enormous pressure, and it isn't always easy to make the right decision. Or even to know what's right and what's wrong."

Good for you, Mom, I thought.

Eighteen

"I don't agree," Shoshanna said. "Lately, I've been thinking that maybe the government's right. Maybe we need to do whatever we can to protect ourselves."

"Not maybe," my grandmother said, delighted that Shoshanna agreed with her.

I was shocked that Shoshanna even had an opinion. She always got a blank look on her face when we talked politics.

"But I do think that Ari has the right to decide for himself," she added. "And I totally understand his decision."

Mimi just shook her head in anger. "You don't know what it's like to live in a country where you can be rounded up and sent to die at any minute," she said. Then she hesitated before going on, and the hard lines around her eyes and lips began to soften. She turned away from us, isolating herself in some painful memory. "There is no place else for us," she said, finally.

Even though Mimi and I hadn't looked at each other once during the entire dinner, I looked at her then. It was only when she talked about her past that I could see a crack in her armor. So, despite what she had said to my parents, and despite what she had done to me, I felt sorry for her. Though I don't think she ever felt sorry for herself—or for anyone else. She could be really tough. For her, there was only one truth. Hers. And if you crossed her big time, well—she might just pretend you never existed. That's what happened with my grandfather.

Mimi met him after World War II in a displaced persons camp in Europe. He'd been in Auschwitz, too. They came to Isreal, got married, and had my mother. But then he decided to go back to Germany when my mother was still a little girl. Mimi never spoke to him again. She never talked about him, either. It was just as if he totally disappeared off the face of the earth. Nobody ever mentioned his name, not even my mother.

"I'm sorry, Mimi," Shoshanna said. "I know we can never really understand what it was like for you."

"No, you can't," Mimi responded. "Which is why we need to do everything possible to make sure it never happens again."

We all silently agreed to allow Mimi to have the last word on this. She was right, of course. We do need to do everything we can to make sure it never happens again.

We just didn't agree about what was included in "doing everything we can."

CHAPTER

19

The next morning when my mother went to check on Shoshanna and Mimi, and my father went to the hotel dining room to get some breakfast, I walked down the path to the stables. I pushed 9 on my cell phone and hoped Maha would answer. I needed to hear an objective voice of sanity. I needed to tell Maha about what had happened between Mimi and me.

When Maha said hello, I spilled out my guts to her.

"I can understand why you're so upset," she said. "The slap was completely unexpected. But your grandmother was caught by surprise, too. You shocked her, and she responded without thinking."

"She's the most stubborn woman I've ever met."

"And what else?"

"And the most generous, maybe the smartest, sometimes the funniest," I said, reluctantly.

"I know she hurt you—probably your feelings more than your face—and I'm not saying that what she did was right. But she's your grandmother, so you have to find a way to get past what happened between you."

Maha was right. Eventually we would all get past it. But I wasn't ready to let go of my anger yet.

By the time we were back on the road, the tension in the family had mostly disappeared. There were still some hurt feelings and a little anger underneath the pleasant chatter, but at least for the moment those feelings remained bottled up.

When we got back to Netanya, we unloaded the car, crammed into the elevator, and rode up to the top floor. Mimi's apartment was filled with light and life. There were always fresh flowers everywhere. But that day, the flowers were bigger and brighter than usual, as if the first poppies and red chrysanthemums of the season promised to compensate for our frustrations, and, yes, for our sadness as well.

All of the furniture in Mimi's apartment was French. Antique. And so was Mimi's jewelry. Once I asked my mother why Mimi wore so much jewelry. "It's kind of embarrassing," I said. "A pair of small diamond earrings isn't so bad, but does she really need a necklace and a bracelet to match?"

"Maybe you shouldn't be so judgmental," my mother said. "Sometimes people have their reasons for doing things the way they do, even if it isn't the way we'd do them. Mimi's family was very wealthy. The Nazis took everything. The furniture, the jewelry, the art. But more important, they took away her parents and brothers and sisters," my mother explained. "She can't replace her family, but she can replace everything else. Maybe not with the same pieces, but with similar things. I think they bring her comfort."

I was thinking about that conversation with my mother as I got dressed for the seder. Mimi and I had continued to shy away from each other. It wasn't that we hadn't spoken since we were at Vered ha-Galil; we had. But our conversation was about unimportant things. It was as though we were both pretending that the slap hadn't happened. Of course, we both knew that it had, and the memory of it kept rushing back at me at unexpected moments.

On some level, I realized that the slap wasn't meant exactly for me. I was the one who had given Mimi the bad news. But I think she was mad at Ari at that moment. And at my mom. And at the Palestinians. She was mad and maybe afraid. Afraid there would be no soldiers in Israel to protect her. Afraid that she'd be carted off again to some unknown concentration camp. So I put my anger and humiliation in a box and kept that box closed tightly when she was around. This isn't to say that the anger never seeped out. It did—a lot. But not when we were together.

"Are you ever going to be finished in the bathroom?" Shoshanna asked.

"Never," I said. "But you can come in if you want to."

"No thanks. I'll wait."

Shoshanna was good at waiting. I'd have burst right in.

"Think they'll be any cute guys at the Seasons?" I asked her when I opened the door.

"Is that all you ever think about?"

"No, sometimes I think about other things."

"Well, you wouldn't know it," she said.

She went into the bathroom and shut the door. Then she opened it again and said, "We're not going to the Seasons Hotel." A minute later I heard the shower.

I opened the bathroom door. "What do you mean, we're not going to the Seasons? That's the best hotel in Netanya. Mimi wouldn't go anywhere else."

"Well, she decided that this year she wanted to attend an old-fashioned religious seder. She wanted us to have the experience."

"You're joking."

"I wish I were. We're going to the Park Hotel."

"She doesn't have anything in common with those people."

I was completely upset. Of all the hotels on Hotel Row, Mimi had picked the last place I'd want to go. We probably wouldn't even get a decent meal there. And I was sure we'd have to sit through an endless seder.

I should probably have started putting on my make-up and getting out my clothes, but I lay down on the bed for a minute. I still had plenty of time. Anyway, I was sure there wouldn't be any interesting guys at the Park Hotel. They'd all be superreligious.

My cell phone rang. I reached into my purse without checking to see who was calling and flipped it open.

"Hey, Noa. *Hag sameah.*"

"Maha?"

"Yeah."

"It didn't sound like you."

"You mean you didn't expect me to call and wish you a happy Passover."

I started to laugh. "Said like a real Israeli."

There was a moment of static tension followed by "Yeah, well. I just called to see how you're doing. You and Mimi."

"We're not exactly okay, but we're better. I'm still mad at her though."

"I thought you said she was the stubborn one."

"Okay. Okay," I said. "Point well taken. We're going to this horrendous seder."

"What do you actually do at a seder?"

"Eat."

She laughed softly, and I started to breathe more easily again. "We have a two minute service. It's mostly about the food at our house. Except this year Mimi made reservations for us at the Park Hotel, and we have to sit through a religious service."

"Groan."

"Exactly."

"So, give me a call when you get back home."

"Remember—you're coming to lunch next week."

"Your mom a good cook?"

"Well, not exactly." We both started to laugh. "But hey, she does cook for Passover. You should come next year. We always invite friends."

We joked around for a few minutes before we hung up. I liked having a Palestinian friend. Then I caught myself. As long as I identified her as my Palestinian friend there would be a subtle barrier between us. Why couldn't she just be my

72

friend? I replayed our conversation and wondered which of us had really created the barrier.

I guess there are all kinds of barriers. The ones between people are sometimes harder to cross. It's a challenge—reaching out to the other side. But as I lay there thinking about her, I dreamed of erasing the barrier between Maha and me. Then I suddenly thought about another barrier I dreamed of crossing—the age barrier between me and Gideon.

When Shoshanna came out of the bathroom, she glanced over at me.

"You asleep?"

"Just thinking."

"About boys?"

"About boy."

"Oh? Something you want to tell me?"

"I have a big crush on Gideon, in case you didn't know."

"Noa!"

"I know. I know."

"Don't waste your time."

"Why not? I've got plenty of time and nothing else to do."

"Yeah, well, don't you know anyone closer to your age?" she asked. She sat down at the dresser and started putting on her make-up. Not that she wore that much.

"Sure, I know lots of guys closer to my age, but they're boring."

Shoshanna shook her head. "You should probably start getting dressed. We're leaving in fifteen minutes, and you know that Mimi will walk out the door at seven o'clock whether you're ready or not."

"You are right about that," I said, and I slipped into a pair of slacks.

Shoshanna turned to look at me. "You're not wearing a dress?"

"I don't have one that fits right. I was going to wear a skirt, but I'm more comfortable in pants."

"Noa, sometimes I think you deliberately try to upset everyone."

"Because I'm not wearing a dress? Get real. The world is in chaos, and you're worried about my wearing pants to the seder?"

"I know the world is in chaos, but there are still certain things you do and don't do. We're not going to seder at a kibbutz. We're going to a hotel. An Orthodox hotel. They expect girls to wear dresses."

I was thinking of a good comeback when Shoshanna's cell phone rang.

She answered it, and I knew right away she was talking to Gideon, so I took my time putting on my sweater and my make-up—which consisted of a little mascara and lipstick. I felt as if I were moving in slow motion when I heard her say, "We can rehearse tomorrow evening. No, we're in Netanya. She's here, too."

Then she handed me the phone. I stared at it for a minute, my mouth wide open.

"Thought you had a crush on him," Shoshanna whispered. "Here's your chance."

"Gideon?"

"Hi," he said. "I just wanted to wish you a happy Passover."

I wanted to think of something clever fast. "I'm not sure how happy it'll be. I'm about to piss everyone off." Damn. That wasn't what I meant to say.

"Sounds good to me," he said. "Wish I were there."

"Me, too. You could take some of the heat off of me."

Pretty soon we were into this great conversation. Shoshanna was completely dressed and pointing to her watch, but I wasn't paying any attention.

When my mother knocked on the door and told us that it was time to go, I said "hold on" to Gideon and told everyone to go on ahead. I'd be there in a few minutes.

Shoshanna shook her head, disgusted.

"It's two blocks away. I'll leave in a minute," I whispered. "Go. Go."

Shoshanna mouthed, "Say good-bye, Noa." Then she turned and walked out of the room, leaving the door open.

I heard the apartment door slam shut, and I was on my own. It almost felt like a date. We began to flirt. I would have given anything not to go to that seder, but I realized that I'd better. "Listen," I said, "maybe I'll come to the rehearsal tomorrow with Shosh."

"Great," he said.

"I better run now, or I'll really piss everyone off."

"As long as they're already going to be pissed, what's the hurry?"

I grinned. "You've never met my grandmother."

"Looking forward to it," he said.

"You really are fearless."

"What do you mean? I'm just a nice, quiet, unassuming guy. Grandmothers love me," he said, laughing.

It was beginning to drizzle, but I took my time getting ready to leave. I wasn't in the mood to hurry to the Park Hotel. I wanted to keep the conversation with Gideon alive for as long as I could.

It was a quarter after seven. I walked out of the apartment and headed for the elevator, going over every word Gideon and I had said to each other. I thought that I had carried off the conversation pretty well.

As I got close to the corner, I was thinking about seeing Gideon the next evening and worrying about what to wear. Suddenly, I heard a huge blast. I jumped back and looked all around me. For a moment I was totally confused. I half-expected to see a bolt of lightening flash across the sky. Then I saw smoke coming from somewhere on the next block. My stomach spun around, and my knees turned to jelly. But a moment later, adrenaline flooded through me and I started walking again. Faster. Then running. I wanted to get to Hotel Row. And I didn't want to get there. I was afraid of what I might find.

I turned the corner. People were milling around in a daze outside the Park Hotel. They were screaming and moaning. They were bleeding. Their faces were covered with soot. Their clothes were torn. Some were limping and crying. A few fainted. My heart was racing. I was totally panicked. I wasn't sure where to turn or what to do.

People from the neighborhood were running toward the hotel yelling, "What happened? Was it a suicide bomber?"

Oh no. It couldn't be. It couldn't be. Without thinking, I crashed through the crowd. I knew, and I didn't know. I didn't want to know. My throat was so tight, I could barely breathe. But the weird thing is that even while I was running through the smoky lobby of the hotel, I was thinking that everyone was really going to be angry at me for being late.

I stopped at the entrance to the dining room—what was left of it. Black horriblesmelling smoke filled the air. The smell almost knocked me over. I gagged, then struggled to keep myself from vomiting. It was dark in the room, but in the faint light from the lobby I could see that the place was a complete mess. The ceiling had collapsed and twisted metal and debris sprawled everywhere. Chairs and tables were upside down. Broken glasses and dishes littered the floor, and the windows had been totally blown out. The overhead sprinklers were working, drenching everything. Injured people were struggling to find their way out as I was pushing my way in. We were ankle-deep in water.

"Mommy!" I screamed at the top of my lungs. I was shaking uncontrollably. I tried not to look at the mangled bodies. "Daddy! Shosh! Mimi!" I screamed their names over and over again as the firemen and the police rushed in.

CHAPTER
20

I waded back through the lobby, through water streaked with blood. My heart was racing. I could barely keep myself from throwing up. The smell from the dining room was horrible. I kept gagging, then breaking out into a cold sweat. Someone walked toward me carrying a large flashlight. Splashes of blood dotted the floor, the ceiling, the walls. It looked as if a bunch of kindergarten kids had attacked the room with finger paints. People lay on the ground, crying for help. A few didn't speak or cry. Even though I'd never seen a dead body before, I knew they'd never say anything again.

Confused, horrified, aware and unaware of what I was doing, I turned to run out, but I slipped, and my foot caught on someone's arm. I shrieked.

When I finally staggered out of the hotel, several people, soot-covered and bloody, were lying in the driveway. Ambulances shrieked around the corner, medics pouring out of them before they came to a full stop. All of the sounds—the cries, the moans, the shrieks, the sirens—fused into one huge sound that clamored in my head.

Suddenly I saw my mother, who must have stumbled out of the hotel on her own. She was sitting on the sidewalk. I was so overwhelmed with relief that I could barely speak as I crouched down next to her. Until that moment, I had had no idea that a terrible deep hole had already opened inside of me. A hole that was completely empty, except for one emotion—fear.

She looked at me, not quite seeing me. Then she closed her eyes and fell backward, her head hitting the ground before I could catch her.

I ran for help. Medics were pouring in and out of the hotel, carrying injured people on stretchers and putting them in ambulances. "Please, "I begged one of them. "Please, my mother's passed out over there."

"Sorry. We'll get to her when we can."

He tried to run off, but I grabbed his sleeve. "Now."

He continued walking, pulling me along with him. "We have to take care of the seriously injured first. If your mother could walk out of the hotel, she'll probably be all right."

"You don't understand, "I screamed.

"I understand," he said, brusquely.

I let go of his arm as he walked into the hotel. Defeated, I staggered toward the place where I'd left my mother, but she was gone. Frantically, I looked around for her. Where was she? And where were my father, my sister, and my grandmother?

My head was reeling. I ran back toward the hotel, checking the stretchers being carried out. Then I ran over to an ambulance about to pull away, its siren already blaring. I banged on the back doors. Nobody responded.

I could feel the tears running down my cheeks before I even realized that I was crying. I just stood there, unable to move.

Other people were just as stunned as I was. Some were walking around in circles. Others were just screaming. I didn't know them. I didn't know any of them. And they didn't know me. I was a stranger.

I began wandering around in circles too, looking at every face, hoping three of them would be familiar. I willed myself to go back inside the hotel, but when I tried to enter, policemen were blocking the entrance. "Most of the wounded have already been evacuated. You don't want to go in there," one of them said.

"Yes, I do!" I yelled.

Other people were trying to wedge in past me, but the police stopped them, too.

"The best thing you can do is to go home. Get out of the way, so we can get our work done," the same policeman said. "The hospital will have a list of the victims' names."

"Victims!" I cried

"There were injuries—and some casualties."

And as if to verify what the policeman just said, several Orthodox men wearing yellow vests slipped past him to collect the remains.

"A lot of people were taken to the hospital with injuries," another policeman said. "Some of them were fairly minor. Go back home. Maybe your family's there, worrying about you. If not—if not, try the hospitals."

As soon as he said that, something clicked. I reached into my pocket to retrieve my cell phone. But my cell phone wasn't there. I had left it on the bed in my rush to get out of the apartment.

I stumbled away, inching through the mess, promising myself that this nightmare would end and that everyone in my family would be okay. The policeman was probably right. My family would head back to the apartment. They were probably already there, waiting for me, afraid for my safety. I laughed like an insane person as I ran, already celebrating our reunion in my mind.

I entered the apartment building, which seemed eerie and silent. The lobby was completely empty, as if everyone had suddenly been carted off to another planet.

I saw my reflection in the elevator that took me up to the top floor, and I was horrified. I was covered with ashes and blood. My mascara formed black owl lines around my eyes and ran down my cheeks, and my clothes were torn and bloody. Seeing myself this way frightened me even more, and my promises to myself were all forgotten.

When I got off the elevator, I ran down the hall and banged on my grandmother's door, hoping that someone would answer it. I waited for an eternity, then I banged and banged again and again until my knuckles were bruised and bleeding. Then I slumped to the floor.

Just then the door of an apartment down the hall opened. Dr. Rubin came running out into the hallway. For a crazy moment I thought he'd opened the door for the prophet Elijah, as we do every year at the seder. I half-expected him to say, "We open the door so that anyone in need can enter."

And I started to wail.

"Noa?" he said, as he came running toward me.

When Dr. Rubin spoke my name, I was so grateful that I sprang up and threw my arms around him.

"It's the Park Hotel," I stammered.

"I know. I know," he said, softly. "I'm on my way to Laniado Hospital."

Dr. Rubin's whole family rushed out into the hallway, leaving the door to their apartment wide open. I could see the seder table.

"Everyone's in the middle of their seder," I said, and I started to giggle because that suddenly seemed so bizarre. Israel is a country of news junkies, and only people in Netanya knew what was going on. Everyone else was missing the story of the year. Even people who aren't religious celebrate Passover in some way or other.

My giggles turned into hysteria, which I couldn't control. Dr. Rubin put his arm around me and led me into the apartment. The rest of the family followed. Then a blur of people surrounded me, throwing questions at me, which I couldn't begin to answer.

I started coughing, and the giggles finally subsided.

Dr. Rubin checked to see if I had any cuts or bruises that needed attending. "You're lucky," he kept saying. "Very, very lucky. Not even a scratch."
The whole time the television was droning on. Then suddenly, a grief-stricken newscaster interrupted the program. "A suicide bomber walked into the main dining room of the Park Hotel in Netanya at 7:20 this evening and blew himself up."

Everyone gasped even though this was not a surprise.

"So far we have no idea about the exact number of casualties. But this was not just murder; it was a massacre."

Dr. Rubin took my hand and led me over to the couch. "I'm going to give you something to relax you a little. Then I'm going to the hospital. You stay here. I'll see if I can locate your grandmother and the rest of your family."

Someone's going to help me, I thought. Dr. Rubin will find them. "Thank you," I whispered. By then I had no voice left and very little emotion. "But I don't want you to give me a shot or a pill, or anything else. I'm coming with you."

"Even if they've suffered superficial wounds, they would have been taken to the trauma center at Laniado or possibly Lev Hazahav," he said. "Why don't you stay here and let me check it out? I'll call you the minute I learn something."

But there was no way I was going to stay there and wait for Dr. Rubin to call. I saw him glance at his wife, and I knew what he was thinking.

CHAPTER
21

The Rubins had a key to my grandmother's apartment, and Dr. Rubin waited for me while I ran back to change my clothes. As soon as I walked into the bedroom, I saw my cell phone sitting on the bed. I grabbed it and dialed and re-dialed my mother's cell phone, my father's cell phone, Shoshanna's, and Mimi's. I couldn't get through to anyone, so I ran to the bathroom and washed up quickly, ignoring my reflection in the mirror above the sink. As I slipped off my blood-stained slacks and pulled on a pair of jeans, I let out a nervous laugh. No one would care anymore that I hadn't brought a dress for the seder.

I rushed back to the Rubins' apartment, clutching my cell phone, willing my mother to call me. Everyone was glued to the television. Miriam Rubin nervously glanced at me.

"It's better to know than to wonder," I said. I ran over to the TV and crouched down in front of it.

Hospital emergency phone numbers scrolled across the bottom of the screen. Scenes of the chaos and destruction at the hotel were playing over and over again. "We have a partial list of the injured. Identities of the victims that have been killed will not be publicized until it's confirmed that the families have been informed," the newscaster said.

Holding my breath, I studied the list. But I didn't recognize any of the names.

"Let's go," I said to Dr. Rubin.

As soon as we got into the car, Dr. Rubin turned on the radio. But we didn't learn anything new. Miriam had come with us in case we couldn't find my family at Laniado Hospital.

I kept redialing my parent's cell phone numbers, and Shoshanna's and Mimi's, but I still couldn't get through. And every few minutes I checked to see if there were any messages on my cell phone—even though it was turned on and I would have heard it ring.

The streets were filled with cars and with people trying to hitch rides to the hospitals. I was already a wreck, and Dr. Rubin's driving didn't help.

Twenty-one

Just as he swerved into the parking lot, my cell phone finally rang. My hands trembled as I put it to my ear.

"Noa? Are you okay?" my mother asked. And I started to weep all over again, though I didn't think I had any more tears inside of me. Little did I know that I had lots and lots more.

"I have to stay at the hospital for a few more hours. They think I might have a concussion," my mother said. "But I'm okay. Some cuts and bruises, a few burns—but I'm okay," she repeated, as if to convince herself.

"Daddy and Shoshanna? Mimi? They must be okay, too, if they were with you," I said quickly, though I knew this didn't exactly make sense.

There was a long silence on the other end of the phone.

"Dad and Shoshanna will be in the hospital a little longer," she said.

"Are you just saying that? Are you just trying not to tell me they're— Are they really in the hospital? Are they really just hurt?"

"Just hurt," she said, with a catch in her voice.

I knew something was wrong, but I didn't want to know what it was yet. I wanted to think—even if it was only for that moment—that my family was safe.

"Ari's on his way.

"You got in touch with Ari?"

"I was able to get through to him. I'll see you in the morning."

"I want to see you now. I'm in the hospital parking lot with Dr. Rubin."

"It's very chaotic. There are people everywhere. Four and five in a room. In the hallways. It would be better if you wait until I come home."

"Dr. Rubin will help me find you." I was about to click off when I added, "I love you." Not something I made a habit of saying to my mother.

"I love you very much," she answered.

CHAPTER
22

I nside the hospital, dozens of people stood in long lines, trying to get information about their relatives. Everyone looked as anxious and as panicked as I felt. But the hospital staff was pretty well organized. Dr. Rubin pulled rank, and they quickly located my mother's room number. I was relieved that I wouldn't have to wait in line. But at the same time, I felt sort of weird. It's one thing to cut in line at the bus stop or at the movies. But it felt wrong doing it here. Somehow it felt as if we were all in this together.

Miriam helped me find my mother's room, and Dr. Rubin went off to surgery.

When I walked in, my mother was lying flat on her back. Her head was covered with bandages, and she looked like a mummy.

"It's not as bad as it looks," she said. "I could leave now, but they want me to stay because of the concussion."

Several other women in the room were moaning. They were older women, and they looked dazed.

"Those are just burns," my mother said when she saw me starring at the harsh red marks on her arm. "They'll heal. So will the cuts on my leg."

"Where's Dad—and Shoshanna? Where's Mimi?"

"Someone came to let me know that Dad and Shoshanna are here. On different floors. When Ari gets here, you can go with him to find them."

"I'm going to check on them now. I'll be right back," I said, as I turned to leave the room.

My mother stopped me. "Mimi's gone, Noa."

"Where'd she go?"

My mother didn't answer me for a moment. And in that moment what she had just said clicked. Tears started spilling from my eyes. My cheeks felt cold and wet, but I couldn't move my hand to wipe the tears away.

"Come here. Next to me," she said, quietly.

I walked over to my mother and stood as close to her as I could get without crawling under the covers with her.

"It was so dark in there. I couldn't see anything," she whispered.

Twenty-two

"I know."

"I don't even know what happened to her. Only that she didn't survive."

"But that's why she moved to Netanya," I insisted. "So she'd be safer."

"Yes," my mother said. She sighed. "But there are some things we just can't control."

"Do Dad and Shoshanna know?"

"Dad knows. Shoshanna's in a lot of pain. She's been heavily sedated."

"What kind of pain? What's wrong with her?"

"Burns for one thing. Some bad burns on her arm. But they'll heal."

"She'll be okay?"

"She'll heal. We'll tell her about Mimi in a few days."

"I'm sorry, Mom." I reached down for her hand. It seemed like a pretty pointless gesture, but I didn't know what else to do.

"I was so relieved when I saw you. Then you disappeared."

"You passed out. I went looking for help, and when I came back—"

"I know. They carted me off on a stretcher. Where were you hurt?"

"Me?"

"There was blood all over you."

"I wasn't hurt," I said, turning away from my mother.

"You were born under a lucky star."

Right, I thought to myself. I hadn't been lucky—I'd been talking on the telephone. I wanted to tell my mother that I wasn't even in the dining room when it happened, but I couldn't.

"She was something else—that Mimi," my mother said. And her eyes filled up with tears.

I felt so useless just standing there holding my mother's hand. I didn't know what else to say or do, so like a fool I just said, "I'm so sorry, Mom," over and over again. And she squeezed my hand hard. Maybe that was all she wanted to hear.

I sat down on the bed next to her, and she fell asleep—still holding my hand.

I'm not sure how long I sat there, listening to the noises of the hospital, watching the endless replays of the incident on TV. By midnight I had learned that 22 people had been killed and 159 injured. Mimi's name scrolled across the bottom of the screen again and again. And every time I saw it, a wave of nausea erupted in my stomach. Mimi and I would never have the chance to feel okay with each other again. And when Mimi and the others had left the apartment together, I'd never even said good-bye.

The newscaster announced that the terrorist had simply walked into the dining room of the hotel and detonated the bomb. There had been no guard at the door! My head started to spin. How could that be?

I continued sitting there, staring at the horrific images flickering across the screen, unable to completely take in what I'd just heard. I kept imagining I saw Mimi in the midst of the chaos. I kept wishing I could reverse time.

My cell phone rang. I glanced at my mother, but it hadn't awakened her. Gingerly, I reached into my pocket with my free hand and pulled it out. Maha's cell phone number stared back at me, and without thinking I shoved my phone back into my pocket.

Finally, when I thought my hand was about to fall off, Ari walked into the room. As if sensing his presence in her sleep, my mother opened her eyes. I let go of her hand and ran over to him. And we stood there clinging to each other for a long time without speaking. Then Ari kissed my mom and told her how sorry he was about Mimi. He didn't have to say anything else. It was all there in his eyes.

Mom kept saying his name as if she couldn't believe he was really standing next to her. "I'm so glad you're here. I'm just so glad you're here."

I wanted to find Dad and Shoshanna, but Mom took my hand again.

"Shoshanna's highly sedated. She's in the burn unit. You can't see her yet."

I looked at Ari for support.

"We'll be able to see her in the morning," he said.

"You sure?"

"Yeah."

"They won't let us in?"

"Not yet."

Mom started telling Ari everything that had happened. Everything that she could remember or piece together. The thing is, she said, "we" this and "we" that, and she never mentioned that I wasn't part of the "we." "We got to the hotel about five or ten minutes after seven," she said. And she told him about the chaos, and the screaming, and somehow stumbling out of the hotel looking for all of us. She told him that I'd stumbled out, too. And that I'd found her and lost her again. And I just kept nodding my head in agreement. In a way, it was true. I had stumbled out of the hotel.

At 2:30 in the morning, as I was leaving the room to locate my father, a doctor blew in like a whirlwind, checked my mom's eyes to see if they were dilated, checked her vital signs, then checked her out of the hospital.

My mother, Ari, and I walked to my father's room. All the way there, I kept thinking my mother was hiding something from us. I wanted to ask her what it was, but the words kept getting stuck in my throat. I hate hospitals. I hate the smells and the isolation of disrupted lives.

There were four men crowded into a cubicle large enough for two. Their worried families were hovering around them. Some were talking. Some were crying. A few were laughing nervously. Ari and I were relieved. Except for his bandages, my father looked perfectly normal. But when Ari walked over to hug him, we realized that his left arm was in a cast.

He said he would be fine in a month. There would be scars, but he would be okay. The shrapnel wounds both he and my mother had suffered were minor. He was trying to act like it was no big deal, and we were trying to pretend that we believed him. But I think we all felt weirdly disconnected, like suddenly we were strangers. "How long before—" my father asked Ari.

"Two days—so I can go to Mimi's funeral. But my lawyer thinks I might be offered a desk job or might be released from the army early. They don't seem to know exactly what to do with me," he added, almost shyly.

We were very, very happy about that. When we'd been talking in Mom's room, Ari had said, "It wasn't so bad in prison." But I knew he meant *I couldn't stand being cooped up like an animal.* When he said, "Mom and Dad will be fine," he meant *I hope they're fine because I don't think I can handle anything else right now.*

"I'm glad you're going to be okay, Dad," I said.

"Come here, my little grasshopper," my father said to me. "I'm so thankful that you're all right."

I walked to his side and smiled weakly. "I want to see Shosh," I said. "Come on, Ari, let's go find her."

Dad motioned for me come closer. And when he put his good arm around me, I knew he was going to tell me something I didn't want to hear. "Shoshanna was hurt pretty badly," he said.

I started to scream. "She's dead."

"Shussssh," he said, almost angrily. "She'll be in the hospital for a while. But as soon as it's possible, she'll be transferred to Jerusalem—to Hadassah Hospital."

As soon as he said that, all kinds of thoughts raced through my mind. Maybe a steel girder had fallen on her, and she had lost a leg. Or maybe she was hit on the head and had brain damage. The one thing I didn't think was the one thing that had actually happened.

"It's important that you stay calm when you see her. This is hard for her. It's going to continue being hard for her."

I looked over at my mother, who was standing there with her eyes closed. I looked at Ari, whose jaw was clamped shut, and I realized that everyone knew the truth except me.

"I want to see her," I insisted.

"It's important that you prepare yourself," my mother said.

"For what?" I yelled, angry at her for holding my hand, keeping me in her room, and not telling me the truth. The other people in my father's room stopped talking for a moment. "Just tell me what happened to her," I hollered. I didn't care who was listening.

My mother sat down on the bed beside my father and told me everything. Ari leaned against the wall, barely able to listen, though he was clearly hearing it for a second time.

I was nauseous. My knees got weak, and I thought I was going to fall to the floor. Then I said to myself, if I'm the lucky one, I also have to be the strong one.

CHAPTER

23

B y the end of the next day—or really what seemed like one long, endless day—my father was ready to leave the hospital, and Shoshanna had been moved out of the burn unit. My mother walked down the hall to her room with Ari and me. Then she turned quickly and, without a word, she walked away. I could feel her absence and wanted to back away myself.

Ari and I stood there for a moment, afraid we'd do or say the wrong thing. "Maybe the less we say, the better," he whispered. I knew he meant, the less *I* said the better. I loved him for lumping us together.

There was another patient in the room, but she seemed to be asleep. Ari walked in first, and I slipped in behind him, trying to stay in his shadow until I could adjust to a new reality. The room was darkened, making it easier to cope with the shock of seeing the angry burns crisscrossing my sister's left arm. Her right arm was hidden under the sheet. But she couldn't hide the pain that had made her face so pale and ghostly looking.

I'd like to say I was totally cool and handled the situation with ease. After all, my parents had warned us. But seeing my sister and hearing about her were two totally different things.

I stayed behind Ari as long as I could. Aside from muttering, "Hi, Shosh, I'm so sorry," I didn't say a word.

Ari kissed Shoshanna on her forehead, then pulled up a chair next to the bed, but I stayed close to the door, easing it open with the toe of my shoe. The room smelled antiseptic, and tears stung my eyes because I felt weak with guilt. I wanted to look at my sister. I wanted to pretend that everything would be okay, but I could barely force myself to glance in her direction.

The first thing I thought was poor Shoshanna. The second thing was that I'd like to kill the person who did this to my sister. Only he was already dead. So I wanted to kill someone else. Someone who might do this to another innocent person I love. I wanted to buy an M16 and pick off a few of those stone-throwing terrorists before they got the chance to strap on bombs and ruin the lives of entire families.

"I was so worried about you," Ari said. "I'm so glad you're alive."

"I'll never be able to play the violin again," Shoshanna said.

"I wish I could say something to make you feel better. I wish I could do something," Ari said. He was quiet for a moment. Then he put his left hand on her good hand. "But there is one thing—I know you. I know how strong you are, and I know that if you can't play the violin, you'll find something else you feel passionate about."

Shoshanna smiled weakly. "What will I do with my time? All these hours and nothing to fill them."

"You need to rest so you can heal. After that you'll find lots of things to fill your time. You'll go back to school, decide what you want to do, and be as busy as ever."

But not as happy, I thought.

"You're right," she said, without much enthusiasm. "My friend Ruthie was a dancer before— Now she's back at school. She's coping. You saw her, Noa."

I nodded, remembering how I could barely look at Ruthie when we met her at the café in what seemed like another life.

Shoshanna winced in pain and reached for the buzzer to call the nurse.

"It's time for my trip to lala land," she said, trying to make a joke. "I'm sure I'll be a regular drug addict by the time I get out of here, which is not so bad, believe me."

"I know what you mean," Ari said. "If it doesn't help one pain, it takes care of another."

I looked at him, not sure exactly what he meant.

"We'll let you sleep now," Ari said, as he leaned over and kissed her on the cheek.

I started to breathe more easily, relieved we had an excuse to leave. I wanted to get away from there as fast as I could before I threw up. "We'll see you tomorrow," I said, inching out the door.

A nurse walked into the room. "Okay," said Shoshanna.

"Can't they do anything about her hand?" I asked Ari as soon as the door swung shut behind us.

"I don't think so. The fingers on her right hand were totally crushed."

"You mean she'll never be able to play the violin again?"

"She wouldn't be able to hold onto a bow."

My mind raced. What other instrument could she learn to play? You need all of your fingers to hold a bow or pound the keys on a piano or pull the strings of a harp.

Twenty-three

The stab of pain I felt at that moment took my breath away. Shoshanna's violin would remain unplayed and unheard forever. There would be no music to help heal our wounds.

CHAPTER
24

On the way to the cemetery, my parents, Ari, and I learned that the death toll from the Passover massacre had reached twenty-eight. We also learned the name of the terrorist— Abdel-Basset Odeh. He had lived within walking distance of Netanya.

We stood at the grave, among all of Mimi's friends and employees. And among all our friends from Jerusalem who had found their way to the cemetery. The teachers from my mother's school, the people who had been in my father's army unit. Matti and his family. Sarah and her whole family. Sarah came up and hugged my mother, my father, Ari, and me as soon as she saw us. She was crying. She said she was sorry, so sorry. I wanted to hug her back, I wanted to talk to her, I wanted to scream and cry. But I just stood there, stiff as a board, numb. I wanted to tell her a million things—except the truth. So I didn't trust myself to say anything at all. She looked at me for a long time, then squeezed my arm gently and walked away.

My mother's eyes filled up with tears; then she whispered, "You think there's always time to make things right."

I moved closer to her and touched her hand. I wanted to put my arm around her, but I felt too guilty, and I couldn't do it.

Lots of people spoke because Mimi was a prominent woman in town. There were laughter and tears. Memories. And what I learned about my grandmother made me very sorry that I hadn't really known her. But it was too late. No matter how her friends and employees praised her, I could still remember the humiliation I felt when she slapped me across the face. Even though I understood why she had done it, that slap was what I remembered most about her.

We were getting ready to lower the body when Ella, my grandmother's housekeeper, said she wanted to say something, despite the fact that she had promised my grandmother she would never reveal her secret. My brother and I looked at each other, totally shocked. People had said many surprising things, but we couldn't imagine what secret Mimi would have told Ella.

"I come here from Russia twenty years go," she began. "I come with six-year-old boy, Dimitri, but with no father or husband."

Twenty-four

Ella may have immigrated to Israel twenty years ago, but her Hebrew was still rudimentary. Her son, Dimitri, was a different story. Everybody thinks he's brilliant.

"I go to work for Geveret Krause, and she teach me Hebrew. I don't learn too good, but she have patience for me. That is not secret I speak of, though most of you probably do not think of her as patient woman."

Everybody laughed softly. And my mother wiped a tear from her eye.

"Secret is that Geveret Krause is most generous woman. When Dimitri finish high school, she call him to her office and tell him she sends him to college. Everything paid. Then she sends him to medical school. Everything paid. Only two rules. He not tell anyone, not even his mother. And he be good doctor. Dimitri break first rule and tell me, but no one else know. She give Dimitri great gift. Now I give her family gift—to know that their Mimi was very good and generous woman."

Everyone was stunned. And when people swarmed around us to offer their condolences, I reached for Ella, and she folded me into her arms.

"Thank you," I whispered.

"Is okay," she said.

"Is okay now," I said.

I drove back to the apartment with the Rubins, who had set up food for everyone. By the time we got there, the apartment was filled with people. Sarah was there with her family. Our eyes met, and she started to cry, so I turned away and noticed Dahlia and Abed standing near the door to the kitchen. Then I saw Maha standing next to them. There had been so many mourners at the funeral that I hadn't seen them there.

Maha had left a half a dozen messages for me. I hadn't answered her first call, when I was with my mother in the hospital, but she had left a frantic message, saying that she had just seen the news and was terrified for me and my family. In her second message, she begged me to call her and let her know that we were all right. Her third message said that she had read the names that had scrolled by at the bottom of the TV and had seen Mimi's. The fourth message offered condolences from her and her family. The fifth said she knew we were in mourning and wondered if we weren't supposed to phone people during this time. Her last one said, "Just wanted to let you know that I'm thinking about you."

I had been thinking about her a lot. I had thought about calling her every day since Passover. I even had conversations with her in my imagination. And in a way, her words had consoled me, but they were only imaginary words. What did she really know about me? How could she really know me? And how could I really know her? We were different. Too different. I didn't want to hear her defend the terrorist who had killed Mimi. I didn't want to hear her say that his anger had driven him to despair. Not that she would have agreed with what he had done. She wouldn't have. But she would have avoided saying he was a Palestinian. She would have avoided the issue of his being a Muslim. And each avoidance would have erected another barrier between us.

I cringed as I saw Maha's brown eyes glaze with tears. She broke away from Abed and Dahlia and headed toward me.

"Noa, I am so sorry—so sorry," she said. "My family sends their deepest sympathy."

She tried to put her arms around me to console me. Maybe to console both of us. Without thinking, I backed away, and she just stood there for a moment. But I saw a flicker of hurt in her eyes before she turned and hurried across the room.

CHAPTER
25

We observed the seven days of mourning after Mimi's death. Even after the mourning period was over, we had very little interest in packing up her apartment—or even thinking about it. The feeling that she was actually gone was still too new. We accepted it sometimes. Other times we half-expected her to walk in the door. Most of the food our friends and neighbors had brought was left uneaten. But sometimes in the middle of the night I'd be famished, and I'd run into the kitchen and gobble up four or five pieces of cake. Then I'd feel sick to my stomach for the rest of the night. In a way I didn't mind feeling sick. It gave me something to think about.

We stayed in the apartment, going back and forth to the hospital every day to see Shoshanna. It got easier for me. Either that, or I got more numb. My body would walk into the room I'd shared with Shoshanna, leaving my emotions behind.

My mother met with the vice president of Mimi's company, and they made decisions about the business. My mother promised she wouldn't sell it, that she would turn the running of the business over to Mimi's associates. She said Mimi would have wanted it that way.

Ari had returned to prison right after the funeral, and by the end of the second week, we were told that Shoshanna could soon be transferred by ambulance to Hadassah Hospital. She had already begun some light physical therapy, which would continue for a long time after the burns on her arm actually healed.

My mother kept glancing at her watch. It was late Friday afternoon, and we were on our way back from the Laniado Hospital. In two days Shoshanna would be released to Hadassah Hospital, not far from our house in Beit Zeit. I was thinking about how hard all this must be on my mother. Then it dawned on me that she seemed to have settled into this alternative life with more ease than the rest of us. I realized that I didn't have a clue about what was going on in her mind, although I sometimes heard her late at night, drinking coffee in Mimi's kitchen.

If anything, my mother seemed more open than usual. Out of nowhere, she would suddenly begin telling me stories about when she was a child. But the strangest thing was what she said about Shoshanna. First she said she wished her own fingers had been crushed and her arm had been burned, rather than Shoshanna's, which I guess most mothers would say. But then she said God must have another plan for her. God! What was that supposed to mean? And who was this so-called plan for—her or Shoshanna?

We aren't a religious family. Far from it. That's why I was so surprised that Mimi had wanted to attend a traditional seder. If we had just done what we usually do—prepare dinner at our house or at Mimi's—we would all be living our lives as usual. So given what happened because we were going to a religious service, it was hard to understand how God had suddenly crept into my mother's vocabulary.

"Why did Mimi decide to go to a hotel this year?" I asked, as my mother glanced at her watch again.

"Her family was observant in France. But after the war, I guess she stopped believing in God. She and my father. I don't think she ever entered a synagogue again."

I glanced at my mother. This was the first time I had ever heard her voluntarily mention anything about her father. I was curious. What was he like? What did he look like? I had never even seen a picture of him. I looked down at my long legs squeezed into the space between the seat and the front of the car. I looked over at my mother's long legs. Mimi had been only five feet tall.

My mother continued. "I don't think we really need them—churches, or mosques, or temples. Or even rituals. But maybe they help remind us that we're not alone."

"Yeah, well, unfortunately, we're not alone. We're surrounded by religious fanatics!"

"Everyone has to find her own truth," my mother said, as if she hadn't heard a word I'd just said.

"Well, my truth is that we ought to get rid of the terrorists. If we have to bomb them into oblivion, then that's what we have to do."

"I'm not sure what the answer is," my mother said, calmly, "but I hope we find a way to live without violence."

"Hope all you want to. It isn't going to happen," I said, angry with my mother for her incredibly naïve attitude. Where was this woman coming from? The concussion she suffered must have affected her brain.

When we got back to Mimi's apartment, my mother barely took time to say hello to my father before she began setting the dining room table. She found a white linen table cloth and put out Mimi's best silver and china. Then she put out Sabbath candles and candlesticks, a small silver wine cup, and a bottle of wine.

Twenty-five

My father and I just looked at each other. A minute later she took a *challah* out of a grocery sack and put that on the table under a fancy, white napkin. She went about her work as if we did this every Friday night. And the whole time she kept checking her watch.

"Made it before sundown," she said, as soon as everything was assembled. "Let's wash up."

Like bewildered sheep, my father and I followed her directions. Then we reassembled at the table, where my mother had poured a little ceremonial wine into all of our glasses. She opened a prayer book.

"*Baruch Atah*," she said, as she lit the candles, something we had never done before on a Friday night. My father and I watched her, as if she were performing in some play to which we'd been invited.

When she finished the prayer over the candles, she picked up the small silver wine cup and started singing the blessing over the wine. She had to stop a few times when she lost her place. But she finished singing, saluted us, and drank the wine. "Pick up your glasses," she said, smiling at us.

We continued the charade. I glanced at my father, who was obviously just as confused as I was.

Then she sang the prayer over the bread. She broke off a piece and handed part of it to me and part to my father and kept a corner for herself. We ate it, and I was almost embarrassed by how pleased she was.

"I'm sorry. I didn't have time to cook," my mother explained, "but I did pick up some soup. I'll just heat it up." And off she went into the kitchen.

"She didn't have time to cook?" I said to my father. "Since when has she ever made soup?" My mother's interpretation of a good soup was opening a few cans and warming them up.

My father raised his eyebrows, not sure how to respond to me or my mother. I couldn't see him going along with the religious stuff. Or me either. Why were we suddenly going back to the dark ages? Life was hard enough as it was.

My mother brought the soup bowls to the table, and we ate in awkward silence. Our family of six had become a family of three. And while my mother seemed to have expanded to fill the void, my father and I seemed to have shrunk.

It felt weird using Mimi's best silverware and dishes. Everything was here, just as she had left it, but she'd never open a drawer again, never sit in her bedroom reading a book, never phone her office for messages. Still, she hovered over the room like a silk shadow, present in everything that she had carefully chosen. I used to study the magical things scattered around the apartment. The art from around the world. The strange books. The Persian carpets. When I was little, I used to sit on the floor and trace the patterns in the carpets till they formed designs in my imagination and opened up spaces for wondrous stories.

I wished I could be that child again.

CHAPTER
26

The first day back at school felt like the first day of kindergarten when you already know most of the kids, and even the teacher. The people were familiar, but the situation was different, and seemed strange.

Everybody knew what had happened and why I hadn't come back to school after vacation. Even though all of my friends and their families and even some of the teachers had come to the funeral, I still felt uncomfortable when I walked through the door.

Ronit, the guidance counselor, put her arm around me and led me to her office. She said how sorry she was and suggested that I drop in to see her after school. I told her I wanted to run the track because I had to get back into shape.

"You can come see me after that," she said.

"I can't. I have a lot of work to catch up on."

She studied her calendar. "What about fourth period, then?"

"English. I don't want to miss that class."

"Well, let's find a time when you *can* come in."

"Ronit, we all talked to a grief counselor in Netanya. I'm fine. If I need to come in and talk to you, I will," I said, confidently. I was lying through my teeth, although I didn't know it at the time.

"Okay," she said. "But maybe it would be good to talk—"

"I talk. I have plenty of people to talk to."

"Good," she said, smiling at me. "Just keep it in mind. If you want to run anything past me, I'm here."

"Thanks. I have to get to my first period class."

The halls were empty as I walked to math class. I didn't want to face anyone. I didn't want people to tell me how sorry they were. Well, I wanted them to, and I didn't want them to.

As soon as I walked in, the room grew completely silent. Then Judith, the teacher, came over to me and took my hand. "We're all so sorry about your family."

I could feel myself blush. I just wanted to get past that first day back, past all the condolences and all the embarrassment. It was just so totally awkward for everyone.

Or maybe it was just awkward for me. Most of the kids in class got up and huddled around me, offering their sympathy. Some of them hugged me. I wanted to tell them that I really didn't deserve it.

At the end of the period Judith called me up to her desk, and I was relieved that I didn't have to walk out with the other students.

"If you need anything, if you need extra time to do your assignments, please let me know."

"Thanks," I said. Then I walked out of the room and headed for my next class, already deciding not to do my homework that night.

It went pretty much the same way until last period—chemistry class. As soon as I walked into the room, Matti came up to me. "I'm glad you're back," he said. "I still can't believe what happened to your family."

"I know."

"It's terrible. But you have to move on, I guess."

"Yeah. I have to move on," I said, as I walked to my stool and pulled it out.

I looked over at Sarah, who had been trying to talk to me all day. I didn't know why I was avoiding her. I knew I should thank her for coming to Mimi's funeral, but I couldn't. I convinced myself that I was waiting for her to apologize for the stupid, little argument we'd had and for her rudeness afterward. I knew, on some level, how ridiculous that was. It was probably the last thing on Sarah's mind and probably should have been the last thing on my mind, too. It wasn't.

"Want to ride after school?" Matti asked, as he sat down on his stool next to me.

"No, thanks. I'm not in the mood today."

We were working on our experiment—I should say, Matti was working on it. I was staring into space when Mr. Drucker came up to me. For a moment I wondered if he was going to bust me for not doing my homework. Then I figured that he was just going to offer his condolences, like all my other teachers.

"I just wanted to remind you of our little talk," he said.

I looked at him as if he'd lost his mind or something. Then I remembered. No excuses for not doing your work. We have choices in life. Well, maybe I would choose not to get a 1 in the class. What's the difference, anyway? I said to myself. So I get all 1s. So I get into Hebrew University. So I work my butt off. So what? My sister practiced the violin every day of her life for hours and hours. Now she can't even run her bow across the strings.

"Sometimes work can be healing," he added.

Yeah, yeah, I wanted to say. Whatever that means. There are some wounds that just won't heal.

He walked away, and Matti and I finished our experiment.

I showered off after track and went outside to wait for my mother to pick me up. She didn't want me to take the bus for a while. But part of me figured what's the difference? If something's going to happen, it's going to happen whether I take the bus or not.

When I saw her car, I sprinted over and got in. Who was sitting in the back seat? Sarah. I didn't say a word to her or to my mother, though they chatted away. Then my mother asked, "How'd it go, Noa?"

I shrugged my shoulders. Even if I had felt like answering her, what could I have said? It was a day that had stretched on endlessly, pulled from one end to the other like a thick rubber band.

When we got home, my mother leaped out of the car. She must have called Sarah. And Sarah didn't want to be here any more than I wanted her to be.

"I've been trying to talk to you," Sarah said. "I don't know why you keep avoiding me."

I didn't say anything.

"I was going to call you while you were still in Netanya, but I wasn't sure you wanted me to. I mean, it seemed like you didn't want to talk to me when we came for Mimi's funeral. Then today, you acted like you were mad at me. Are you still mad at me?"

"No," I said, without much conviction. The whole thing seemed so unimportant now.

"It was a stupid argument," she said. "You were right. What Ari does really is his business. I just felt hurt and disappointed, I guess, and I was so worried about my dad that I couldn't really hear what you were saying."

"Maybe you were right," I said. "I don't mean about Ari's deciding not to serve in the territories. That is his business. But maybe you were right about defending the territories—at least until the Palestinians decide to stop killing innocent people."

Sarah looked at me, shocked. I knew this was a complete turnaround from what I used to say, from what I used to believe. The thing is that I didn't realize I'd changed my mind until that minute. So Sarah wasn't the only one who was surprised.

"So is Ari going to, you know—?" she asked.

"He still refuses to serve in the territories, so he's back in prison. That's all I know."

"Hmmm," she said. And I could tell she was feeling nervous, afraid she'd say the wrong thing.

I wanted things to be like they had been before, and so did Sarah, although neither of us knew exactly how to get back to that place again. It was up to me in a way. I had to be the one to just be myself with her, but I couldn't remember exactly what that felt like.

"Want to do homework together?" she asked, as we got out of the car.

"I don't think so."

"So how about I come in, and we just hang out for a while?"

I didn't really want to hang out, but I figured, what difference did it make?

"Okay."

We slung our book bags down in the front hall, then headed to the kitchen, which was conspicuously empty. We went to the refrigerator and stood there looking inside, as if we'd find the cure for all our sorrows there.

"Mind if I have some cereal?" Sarah asked, as she took out the milk.

"Help yourself."

"Want some?"

"I'm not hungry."

Sarah poured herself some cereal, hesitated for a moment, then walked over to the radio, and turned it on. We always listened to music when we studied together. But the radio was tuned to a classical music station, and as soon as the music came on—a violin concerto—I ran over and snapped it off. Sarah just looked at me.

"I don't want to hear that."

"Okay," she said. "No problem."

Sarah was trying hard not to offend me.

"Are you still mad at me?" she asked again, as she sat there eating the cereal.

"No. Are you?"

"No. I was that day, but I figured that by the next day we'd both be over it. Then you walked right past me the next day and didn't say one word, so I figured you were really mad at me."

"Because you were with Aviva. You didn't even look at me."

"Oh," she said.

She thought about it for a while. Then she added, "I'll apologize if you want me to."

"Whatever. It's not all that important."

"Okay," she said, and I wondered why her apologizing had seemed so important to me at the time.

In a way I was glad Sarah was at my house. We weren't fighting anymore, which was good because she was my oldest friend. But at the same time I wished she would go home. I had a headache. Not exactly a headache, more like an emptiness in my head where my emotions used to be. The phone rang, but I didn't bother picking it up. The machine went on, and we stopped talking.

"Hi, this is Gideon," the voice said.

I looked at the answering machine, but I didn't make a move to pick up the phone. Sarah jumped up from the table and started to reach for it. I shook my head, no, and she sat down again. We avoided looking at each other as we listened to the rest of the message.

"Noa, I'm driving to the hospital late afternoon tomorrow to see Shoshanna. Give me a call if you're free around 4:30 and you want to go with me."

When the message ended, Sarah was almost bursting. "Why didn't you pick it up? This is your big chance. Alone in a car with him. What more could you ask for?"

"I don't know."

"Call him back. Tell him you'll go. You want to see your sister, anyway, don't you?" Sarah stared at me in disbelief.

"I have too much homework to do."

"Do it now. Come on. We'll do it together."

"Nah."

"Come on. You know I can't do the chemistry without you."

"Sarah, what are you going to do when you go to college? I might not be around to help you."

"I don't plan on taking chemistry in college. Now come on. Call him back, then help me with the homework," she said.

"I'll help you with the homework," I said, sighing. "But I'm not going to call him back."

As we lugged our books to the kitchen table, I heard my mother's footsteps.

"Just a minute," I said, and I walked over to the answering machine and erased the message.

Sarah shook her head and looked at me as if I were a complete stranger. And you know what? Maybe I was.

My mother moved effortlessly through the kitchen, making dinner, as Sarah and I started to work. Halfway through the assignment, my mind went totally blank. Sarah thought I was kidding. Chemistry had always been pretty easy for me. But for some reason the homework didn't make any sense. In fact, when I looked at the words, they seemed meaningless.

"I can't do it," I said to Sarah. And I slammed the book shut.

"That's okay. Now you know how I feel when I try to do the homework."

"I'll look at it again after dinner if I have time. Maybe it will make more sense to me."

"I'm sure it will." Sarah laughed. "If it doesn't, we'll both be in trouble to-morrow. Unless—"

"I still have to do my work. Drucker's so tough. I think the man's a biological freak. I don't think he has a heart."

Sarah got up and imitated Mr. Drucker's stiff walk. Sarah can imitate any-body, and usually it cracks me up. I forced a smile.

"Claz," she said with a German accent, "for your next asszinment ve must be careful not to blow up ze whole school." She started to laugh, but suddenly I felt tears running down my cheeks. Sarah slapped her hand over her mouth, horrified by her unfortunate reference.

CHAPTER
27

Eventually, the chemistry made sense to me again. But I didn't go out of my way to do the homework. I figured I could slack off. My teachers would have to average in my grades from before Passover, so I didn't think I'd do all that bad. And I guess I didn't really care what my grades were, anyway.

Actually, I didn't care about most things. Friends would call, but most of the time I didn't want to talk to them. One day my mother signaled to me that Maha was on the phone, but I shook my head and waved, indicating that I didn't want to talk to her. After my mother made some excuse for me and hung up, she looked at me for a long time. She said that it was thoughtful of Maha to come to Mimi's funeral. But it didn't feel thoughtful to me. What right did she have to keep calling? What right did she have to invade the privacy of Mimi's funeral? I spun myself into an angry funk, so I wouldn't have to have to admit that I missed talking to her. She was a Palestinian, just like the guy who had killed Mimi and maimed my sister. Maybe she wasn't out dancing in the streets like lots of other Muslims when they heard the news, but I knew how she really felt. And I didn't want to listen to her talk about what Israel had done in Ramallah in retaliation for the Passover Massacre. Sure, even then, a part of me felt sorry for all of the innocent families whose homes were destroyed. Sorry for all the children scared out of their minds by Israeli soldiers tramping through their kitchens, turning everything upside down and inside out. And before Passover, I would have joined my father to protest Israeli's going to such an extreme, using any excuse to humiliate the Palestinians.

But I was too raw. I didn't want to talk about what we had done wrong. I didn't care! In my mind Maha had become the other, a part of the "they"—as in, because "they" want to destroy us all, it's useless to talk about it. We do what we have to do in order to survive.

We took turns visiting Shoshanna in the hospital every day. I usually went with one of my parents. She got one infection after another, so she had to stay longer than expected. Burn patients suffer more than any other patients, I think. And even though the burns were confined to her arm, she was still in a lot of pain. Sometimes when I walked toward her room, I could hear her groaning softly. Still, she tried to put up a good front. But when she thought no one was looking, I would catch her staring at her useless fingers. It wasn't that they looked so bad; it was just that those fingers would never be able to hold a bow again.

But Shoshanna had been doing physical therapy at the hospital. And all kinds of other therapy, too. Me? I didn't think I needed any therapy. I thought I was just fine.

When I got home from school one Friday, my father was waiting for me with a surprise. His cast was off. The cuts and burns had healed, and he looked like he'd always looked. The last visual reminder was gone. Dad was Dad. Unlike Mom who had become a religious fanatic. Okay, maybe fanatic is an exaggeration. But the woman read the Bible every day. Of course, it amused my father.

"Looking good," I said. "You want to box?"

"Can't do that. But tell you what—go change your clothes and I'll race you down to the main road and back."

"You? You'll race me? You gotta be kidding."

"You're out of shape, girl. I can beat you now."

"Oh yeah. Sure you can."

"Try me."

"I know what you're trying to do," I said. But I was kind of pleased. I hadn't run since that first day back at school—after the incident. I *was* out of shape. And if anyone else had challenged me, I probably would have made up some excuse. I wasn't planning to participate in the Maccabee races this year, anyway.

"Not too subtle, am I?" he said, and he laughed.

I laughed, too. "I'm going to put on my running shoes. I'll be right back."

I ran to my room, humming to myself, something I hadn't done in a long time. I kept humming as I pulled my hair back into a ponytail and changed out of my sandals into my running shoes.

"Let's do it," I said, as I walked back into the kitchen. "Loser has to listen to Mom talk about the Bible portion of the day."

"That'll spur me on," my father said under his breath. Then he looked sort of embarrassed.

"Don't worry. I won't tell her you said that."

As we raced to the main road, the endorphins kicked into gear. I started to fly, leaving all the hurt and anger of the past month behind me. I raced faster and faster, my feet barely touching the ground. Even though I was out of shape and breathing heavily, I pushed myself to go on. I hit the road and turned around to run back, passing my father, who was panting so hard I was afraid he'd have a heart attack. But I kept going. I couldn't stop. I was running again. I was laughing and running.

Halfway back up the road, I hit a metaphorical wall and almost collapsed. But I forced myself to keep going. I wasn't racing my father any more. I was racing my inner demons.

When I got to the house, I did a little dance. Then I stretched my leg muscles and fell into a kitchen chair. Fifteen minutes later, my father trudged into the kitchen. His face was so red, he looked like he was on fire, and the sweat was pouring out of him.

"I almost had you," he said, though he could barely breathe.

We both laughed.

Then just like that, he said, "Did Mom tell you that Shoshanna's coming home from the hospital tomorrow?"

"Celebration!" I yelled. Then I felt sort of scared. I wasn't sure how to act. I wasn't sure Shoshanna would be up to celebrating.

"We have to decide what to do about her violin," my father said.

"What do you mean?"

"Should we put it away somewhere?"

"No! Put it in our room where she can look at it and imagine hearing the music she used to play."

"Mom thinks we should put it away."

"If Shoshanna wants to put it away, that should be her choice. But we can't pretend it doesn't exist."

"Yeah. I think you're right," my father said. "We can't pretend it doesn't exist."

CHAPTER
28

Mom had painted our room sunshine yellow, and when Shoshanna walked in she was surprised and delighted. She looked around and smiled. She looked at the dressers and the book shelves. She looked at everything except her violin case in the corner.

"I've made your favorite meal," Mom said to her.

"You picked up some eggplant parmesan at the supermarket?" Shoshanna said, without a hint of sarcasm.

"I made it," Mom said.

"Mom's a cook now."

"Anything will taste better than the hospital junk."

"No. I mean it. Mom's really cooking."

"Let's eat, then," Shoshanna said, smiling. At least, she was trying to smile.

It was strange having Shoshanna at the table with us after all this time. I wished Ari were there, too. I think we were all a little nervous. I know I was.

Then somehow we got to talking about Mimi. Mom brought the conversation around to her a lot those days.

"My mother could do anything. She could make soup out of stones."

"Mimi was dynamite, Mom, but I think you're exaggerating," I said.

"Well, maybe I'm exaggerating a little. But when we were struggling—before she got her beauty product going—she'd gather some greens, some this and some that, and *voila*—a delicious soup."

"Did Mimi speak French to you when you were little?"

"She did at first. But unfortunately, I refused to answer her if she spoke to me in French. Actually, she spoke French, English, and Hebrew, all very well."

"She could swear in four languages," my father said. "Don't forget. She could also swear in German."

We all laughed and took turns repeating some of Mimi's choice expressions. And for that moment, none of us thought about the bombing. We were all just laughing.

Twenty-eight

"You must have gotten your language genes from Mimi," Shoshanna said to me.

"Yeah, but I can't swear in four languages. Only three."

"Noa's English is very good," my father said. "She has almost no accent."

"How would you know?" I said, teasing him. "Your accent's terrible."

"Too bad Noa doesn't do her homework," my mother said. "She could get a 1 in that class."

I gave her a look. "How do you know I haven't done my homework?"

"I spoke with Ronit this morning. She said you haven't been coming in to see her for counseling, either."

"I don't need counseling," I said, angrily. And the mood in the room changed just like that.

"I know it's been difficult for you, but your finals are coming up. You're way behind in you school work."

"Stop criticizing me. You don't know," I yelled.

My mother looked stunned for a moment. Then she said, "Where is that anger coming from? It wasn't meant as a criticism."

"Yes, it was," I said. "And you're the one who made me angry."

"Noa," my father said. I thought he was going to say something to appease me. But he didn't. He said something that shocked me, instead. "Noa, after your mother spoke with Ronit, she phoned a psychologist. Even though we all talked to someone right after Passover, we thought we should see someone else now."

"Why now?"

"I think we all have things that haven't been talked about. Maybe we need to discuss them as a family. Maybe there are things that still bother us or make us angry."

"Like?" I said, shaking.

"Like the fact that I still have bad dreams sometimes."

"Then you go!" I said. "I'm not having bad dreams."

"Mom thinks we should all go."

"My therapist thinks it might be a good idea to see someone—as a family," Shoshanna said, quietly.

CHAPTER
29

A little over a week after Shoshanna came home we met with Dr. Freud. I was hoping my parents would cancel the appointment. I'd been on my best behavior all week, and everything seemed to be running pretty smoothly. But they didn't cancel.

His name isn't really Dr. Freud, of course. It's Dr. Fried, but I liked to call him Dr. Freud. It irritated him, even though he pretended it didn't.

My father was telling him about his nightmares. And Dr. Freud was nodding, his head bobbing up and down like he was a puppet and someone was pulling his strings. It was all I could do to stop myself from laughing. In the past—before Passover—if Shoshanna and I had been in a situation like that we would have looked at each other and known what each other was thinking. Then I'd start to laugh uncontrollably, and she'd just sit there calmly as if she had no idea what was going on.

I looked at her then, but she wasn't looking at me. She wasn't looking at anyone.

"If only I could have done something differently," my father was saying. "If only I had been quick enough, I could have thrown myself in front of Shoshanna. Saved her."

"You did throw yourself in front of her," my mother said.

My father looked at her, totally astonished. "No, I didn't. I fell to the ground, and the beam struck both of us."

"You fell to the ground after you dashed in front of her," my mother insisted. "You tried to push her out of the way. That's why—that's why—"

"Go on," Dr. Freud said.

"That's why Shoshanna is alive," my mother said.

Suddenly, my father got this look on his face—like something had hit him and he was about to crumble. His chin began quivering, and the lines on his forehead bunched together in the middle of his face. But he was smiling. And all the time, tears kept pouring out of his eyes. Then he just took a deep, deep breath and let it out very slowly. My mother reached over and took his hand. There were tears in her eyes, too. "Thank you," he said to her. My mother squeezed my father's hand. Then she reached over and wiped away his tears.

I glanced over at Dr. Freud. He was nodding his head at my parents, like he was blessing them. Then he turned toward Shoshanna.

"Did you realize that your father saved your life, Shoshanna?"

"No. It was all a blur."

I looked at her, surprised she was answering him. It almost felt as if she were betraying me by being so civil.

"What hurts most?" Dr. Frankenfreud asked. "The physical pain or the loss?"

She looked at him for a long moment. And he looked directly at her. If Dr. Freud had known Shoshanna before, if he had heard her play the violin, he wouldn't be asking her what hurt most. I felt like shouting, "What do you think hurts most, freako?"

"I'm not sure," Shoshanna answered, quietly. "I can't help thinking about the physical pain. I go to the hospital for physical therapy twice a week. And I've talked about my feelings of loss with the psychologist, but not exactly in those terms."

"Have you seen any of your friends yet?" he asked.

"Just a few of the people I met at the hospital. And one friend."

"And other than coming here and to the hospital, have you gone out of the house in the week you've been home?"

"Not really."

"May I ask why?"

The man was completely insensitive.

"I'm not ready to face them yet," she answered simply and honestly.

"I understand," he said. Then he looked at each of us separately. "We have to end our session soon, but I'd like to ask you all a question before you leave. What's changed most for you in the aftermath of the incident?"

"I've begun going to religious services," my mother said. "Of course, I miss my mother, and her absence has left a great hole in my heart. Not a day goes by when I don't think about her. But I also tell myself we can choose to dwell on the horrible things that happened to our family, or we can choose to thank God for saving some of us."

Well, that *is* what's most different about my mother, but what's also different is the way she acts since she became religious. She walks around half-dazed with calm, like the old Yemenite woman who lives across the road. It's she has these superhuman powers. She used to complain all the time if we didn't help her around the house on days when the *ozeret* didn't come to clean. Now she never even asks us to help. She just does everything herself. And more than she used to, like cooking. We've never eaten so well.

Almost every Saturday, she hurries off to some kind of religious service, which is a blessing, I guess. She could have gone all the way and become really religious, shaved her head and worn a wig, taken up wearing those shapeless, long dresses, the whole works, the way the ultra-Orthodox do. But she hasn't lost her mind completely—yet.

"What's most different about my life," my father said, "is my lack of trust. I used to trust everyone. Now it's difficult for me to trust any stranger."

"Yes," Dr. Freud said, "I understand."

"You know what's changed in my life," Shoshanna said.

"I know that many things have changed," Dr. Shrink said.

"You're right." She hesitated for a moment. "Even though Beethoven was nearly deaf at the end of his life, he could still compose music. He could hear it in his imagination. But he was an old man, and he'd had many years to perfect his craft. I still had a lot to learn. But—" She paused and took a deep breath. I think we all did. "But I'll never be able to play my violin again," she said quietly, almost as if she were saying it to herself. "I still hear the music in my head, but playing music was the most important thing in my life, so I guess you could say that I've simply lost all hope."

She said this without any tears, as a statement of fact, but I know how much it must have hurt her. My own stomach spun around, and I could feel angry tears building up inside of me. I wanted to run out of the room, screaming. Instead, I bit the inside of my bottom lip and just stared straight ahead.

"Thank you, Shoshanna," Dr. Freud said. "That must have been very difficult for you to say."

She closed her eyes and nodded.

I should have put my arms around her, told her how much I loved her. But I wasn't ready to be honest with anyone then. Including myself. And I wasn't about to give an inch to Dr. Freud.

"Noa?" he asked, turning to me.

My jaw locked into place for a moment and I glared at him. "Nothing's changed," I snapped. "Nothing's changed in my life, at all. Nothing happened to me. I'm perfectly fine. This is a waste of time for me."

"So you think it's a waste of time?"

"I don't *think* it's a waste of time. I *know* it's a waste of time. Maybe not for my family, but it is for me."

"I understand that you used to be a very good student," Dr. Freud remarked casually, as if he hadn't been paying attention to a word I said.

"Yeah."

"And how are your grades now? It's almost the end of the school year, isn't it?"

"If you know I was a good student, then you probably know that my grades are not 1s now. In most of my classes, they're not even 2s."

"Ah," Dr. Freud said. "You're a very clever girl to figure that out."

Oh, come on, I thought. Stop treating me like I'm ten years old.

"And you're a very clever doctor for getting me to talk, but that's all I'm going to say."

"That's all right," he said. "You don't have to say anything if you don't want to."

He just had to get in the last word. But I was not about to let that happen. "I don't want to say anything," I insisted.

CHAPTER
30

Sarah was sitting in front of the door when we got back from the inquisition. Things still weren't the same between us. She continued to pretend I was her best friend. And she came over all the time, so we could do our homework together, homework that I had no interest in doing. I wanted her to disappear from my life like my so-called friend Maha had. Maha had stopped calling me, of course, but I had convinced myself that if she had really been a friend, she would have persisted even though I never called her back. Part of me knew that what had happened to Mimi and Shoshanna wasn't her fault; another part of me blamed her anyway.

My mother had been embarrassed every time she had told Maha I would call her back, because she knew I wouldn't. She appealed to my father, but he didn't put much energy into backing her up. It would have been hypocritical, since he'd been busy avoiding Abed's calls.

So, of course, we didn't invite Maha to visit. And though my father and I never discussed it, there was a covert understanding between us that we had spent enough time worrying about the suffering of the Palestinians.

Abed stopped calling, too, and one day his horse was gone from our backyard. But Sarah just wouldn't take the hint.

"Hi," she said almost meekly when my family and I got back from Dr. Freud's. It was as if she weren't quite sure I'd respond. I admit it. Sometimes I didn't say hi back. Sometimes I didn't feel like it. And sometimes I just couldn't.

"Having trouble with chemistry?" I asked, half sarcastically, as we walked toward the house.

"Why do you talk to Sarah that way?" my mother whispered.

I didn't answer her. My father put his arm around me, but I shrugged it off. They're all so weird, I thought, sitting in some stranger's office telling him how they feel. If my father didn't trust strangers anymore, why did he trust Dr. Freud? Well, Dr. Freud helped him a little, I guess. But maybe it was just a matter of timing. Eventually, my parents would have had that little discussion, anyway.

"My father said we could hop a bus ride with him and go into town and have dinner or something," Sarah said. "Then come back with him later."

For a minute I almost wanted to do that.

"That's a great idea," my mother said. "Go, Noa."

This shocked me since my mother drove me to school and back every day now and insisted I stay far away from public places.

"Not today," I said.

"Okay," Sarah said, looking upset. "Then maybe you can help me with chemistry."

My parents and my sister went into the house, but I lingered outside, hoping that Sarah would finally get the hint and go home.

"I haven't been doing that well in class lately," she said, "and it's nearly the end of the semester."

"I've seen you talking to Mr. Drucker after class. Isn't he helping you? Or do you have a crush on him or something?"

"On Mr. Drucker?" Sarah started laughing, and she couldn't stop. "He's almost old enough to be my grandfather."

"Stranger things have happened."

"Oh yeah? What?" she asked, still laughing.

"You have a crush on the wrong person, and your whole life changes," I snapped at her. "That's what!"

Sarah stopped laughing. "I'm trying to be your friend, but I'm getting tired of your moods, Noa."

"Then go home."

"I didn't want to come here in the first place."

"What's that supposed to mean?"

"Nothing. It's just that everybody's worried about you."

Just as I thought. People were talking about me behind my back. If I really cared, I'd be pissed off. What did I have to do to prove that I was fine?

"Everybody? Who's everybody?" I asked, snidely.

"Me. I'm worried about you," she stammered. "But you're making it pretty hard to be around you."

"Like I said, go home."

"You're getting a 3 in chemistry," she hissed, obviously frustrated with me. "So?"

"You have to get yourself together. You're ruining your future."

"Oh, come on. We live in Israel. What future do we have?"

That stopped her for a minute, and it stopped me as well.

"We have to have hope," she said, finally. "We have to believe that things will change."

"They will," I agreed. "They'll change for the worse."

"We're a strong country."

"Not strong enough to protect innocent people from being blown away if they're in the wrong place at the wrong time."

"Sharon will beat them in the end."

I began to marshal my objections to Ariel Sharon, so I could explain to Sarah why our prime minister was such a disaster. But then I remembered Passover. "Maybe," I said.

I sat down on the step and looked at the olive trees across the road in front of the Yemenites' house. The old trees had stood there embracing for hundreds of years, while we humans come and go. Who will live in my house after us, I wondered. "I hope Sharon sends the Israeli Defense Force into the camps and wipes out every last terrorist! If innocent people get killed, I'm sorry, but that's what happens in war."

"That's what my mother says," Sarah muttered.

"My father says he still hopes for a different solution. But he stopped going to Peace Now meetings. And he doesn't even seem to trust one of his best friends."

"I always forget Abed's a Muslim," Sarah said. "I've seen him at your house for as long as I can remember. He's just Abed."

"What if he's not *just* Abed?"

"What do you mean?"

"He's a doctor. He goes into the refugee camps once a week as a volunteer. Maybe he has a secret life. Maybe the terrorists have persuaded Abed to work for them."

"Are you nuts? Abed is a good friend of your family's, and he's a pacifist."

"People change."

"He's been dating a Jewish woman for fifteen years!"

"They never got married. Maybe there's a reason for that."

"Yeah, there's a reason. Her mother said she'd drop dead if Dahlia married Abed."

"How do you know?"

"You told me!"

"God, Sarah, make up your mind. I come around to thinking like you do, and you suddenly become a peacenik."

"You know what? I can't follow your logic. I never could. But somehow things have gotten all twisted up here, and I don't know how or why."

"Whatever," I said, suddenly tired of this discussion.

"So, are you going help me with chemistry or not?"

"Not."

"Then what am I going to tell Mr. Drucker?"

"That you didn't know how to do it. Stay after class tomorrow. He'll help you. He has nothing better to do with his time."

"That's not what I mean."

I looked at her, confused. She looked confused, too, like she'd said the wrong thing and didn't know how to get out of it.

"I gotta go," she said, and she started walking away.

"Sarah! What did you mean?"

I could see all the circuits shorting out in her brain. She gets this look on her face when she tells a lie, or when she can't think of a good enough lie to tell.

"Ummm, he thinks it would be ummm better if we ummm worked—if we did our homework together."

"Better for who?"

"For both of us."

"Why me? I'm the one who helps you." My heart was suddenly pounding, and I was feeling very upset.

"I'm getting a 2 in chemistry," Sarah said, frustrated. "You're the one who's getting a 3."

"So he thinks you can help me raise my grade? That's a laugh. If I did the homework assignments, I'd get a 1."

"Yeah, but you don't."

"That's my business."

"Well, Mr. Drucker is making it my business, too."

I was starting to get the picture, and I wasn't liking it, although I was sort of pleased that Mr. Drucker seemed to care whether or not I got a good grade in the class.

"He's worried about you."

"So he's the 'everybody'?"

"One of them."

"Well, here's your assignment from me. You call tell all the 'everybodies' to mind their own business. I'm just fine."

"Then you'll go horseback riding with Matti and me Saturday?"

"You and Matti!"

"We're just friends."

"Right. No, I won't go horseback riding with you and Matti Saturday or any other day. Now go home, Sarah. Go do your stupid chemistry homework and leave me alone."

CHAPTER
31

" Time passes. You accept. You adjust." Those were the words my mother kept repeating. She hid behind her newly found religion, going to Bible classes, studying Torah, saying prayers to ward off evil spirits. Okay, so I'm exaggerating again. She hadn't quite reached that point yet. But she did arrive home with another set of dishes and flatware one day, and she announced that we were going to keep kosher. What a pain! No milk and meat together at a meal. No mixing the meat dishes and flatware with the dairy dishes and flatware. No shellfish, which means she won't let us bring shrimp into the house. And that's just for starters.

My father went along with the program and said not to make a fuss about it. If it made her feel good, he could accept it. Not that he bought into it at all. He can't even keep the dishes straight. If my mother comes into the kitchen and finds that he's eating a piece of chicken on a dairy plate, she scoops up the dish and the fork and buries them in the backyard. That's what you have to do to make them kosher again. One night it rained unexpectedly, and a whole bunch of flatware made its way into our neighbor's yard.

We were still going to see Dr. Freud, even though it was summer vacation, but I was still just sitting there most of the time. Occasionally, he saw my parents or Shoshanna separately, but not me. He was smart enough to know I wouldn't come even if he begged me to, which, of course, he wouldn't. It's not his style.

I dropped out of debate class before the end of school and stopped running track. My grades weren't great, but I didn't care. This being real life and not a movie, no mechanical god descended from heaven in time to convince me to take an interest in school again. It irritated me that Sarah got a 2 in chemistry, and I got a 3, even after Mr. Drucker factored in my pre-incident grades. But that's life. And anyway, I knew I'd have to report for military duty eventually, and nobody in the Israeli Defense Force would ask me what grade I'd gotten in chemistry.

Ari had been released from detention for Friday night and Saturday, and had come to see Dr. Freud with us. He hadn't changed his mind about refusing to serve in the territories, but the army had offered him a desk job. He hadn't decided whether to take the job or return to prison and continue his protest against the IDF.

Me? If the army had sent me to guard the territories, I would have blasted the hell out of anyone who so much as looked at me.

Dr. Freud said he sensed a lot of anger in me. So? I thought. I have every reason to be angry.

I wandered into the kitchen, led by the smell of soup. "If you're making chicken soup, it must be Friday night," I said to my mother.

"Would you consider changing your clothes for the Sabbath?" she asked me.

"No, I'm comfortable this way."

"Ari's home with us for the first time in months."

I could see how excited she was. She had held his hand during the entire time we sat in Dr. Freud's office. My mother is crazy about Ari. Who isn't? Unlike me, he has a very sweet nature. Mimi used to say that Ari was lovable, Shoshanna was talented, and I was smart. I used to think—poor Ari, he must feel bad just being lovable. Now I'm wondering if she thought he got the best genetic deal.
I took out a spoon—the right one—to taste the soup. It was delicious, and I almost complimented my mother. Then I noticed the table. It was set for six. There were only five of us.

"Not Sarah again," I said. Despite Sarah's not wanting to put up with my so-called moods, she somehow managed to put up with them, anyway.

"Shoshanna's invited a guest for dinner."

"One of the other victims?"

"Stop, Noa. I'm tired of hearing you talk that way. We're all tired of it. One of these days, you're going to slip and say that in front of Shoshanna."

"Well, she is a victim. She just won't admit it."

"She doesn't see herself as a victim."

"Exactly."

My mother shook her head, annoyed with me. That was the usual state of affairs around the house. I told the truth—or what I thought was the truth—and everyone was upset with me.

Two minutes later Shoshanna walked into the kitchen, and I was in total shock. She was wearing a low-cut, black dress with half her anatomy showing. She'd never dressed this way before. Never.

I was just waiting to see if my mother would ask her to change. This was not exactly the proper attire for welcoming the Sabbath. I also noticed for the first time that Shoshanna had a stylish hair cut. She never used to bother with things like that.

My mother just smiled at her. "Will you cut some roses from the yard," she asked, "or shall I ask Dad to do it?"

"I'll do it," Shoshanna said, and she went to the drawer and took out the pruning shears.

After she walked out the patio door, I turned to my mother. "How do you think she's going to cut flowers with her left hand?"

"She's been practicing using her left hand the way she used her right hand before. Haven't you noticed?"

"I guess not."

"Luckily, she already had a lot of flexibility in the fingers of her left hand from playing the violin."

"Yeah, luckily."

My mother decided to ignore the sarcasm, and I was a little embarrassed that I was being sarcastic. I walked out of the kitchen and wandered back toward my bedroom. On the way, I glanced at myself in the mirror hanging in the hallway. My hair, which I hadn't bothered to wash in days, looked greasy, and my shirt was wrinkled and not that clean. My jeans could have used a washing, too. I raised my arm and sniffed under my armpit. Not just my jeans.

Scrubbed and clean for the first time in nearly a week, I was on my way back to the kitchen when I heard a familiar voice. It was Gideon. I turned and beat a retreat to my bedroom. I collapsed on my bed just as I heard my mother's footsteps coming down the hall. She knocked on my door and opened it without waiting for me to invite her in.

"Dinner's ready," she announced. "Gideon's here."

I didn't say anything. She ignored the fact that I was just lying there and turned to leave. "Thank you for changing your clothes," she said, as she walked down the hallway, "and, by the way, your hair looks beautiful."

I ran my fingers though my long curls. It had taken me fifteen minutes just to get out the snarls so I could wash my hair.

I had a dilemma. I didn't want to see Gideon. I had purposely avoided seeing him when I had visited Shoshanna at the hospital. I had never returned his phone call. I hadn't seen him since Shoshanna and I went to his house so they could practice for the concert, which they had never given. In fact, I felt terrified about seeing him, but I didn't know why. At the same time, if I refused to go into the kitchen for dinner everyone would think I was just being stubborn for a reason they couldn't possibly understand. And Shoshanna might think I didn't want to have dinner with them because I still had a crush on Gideon. Which I didn't. I didn't even want to think about him.

I got up and marched into the kitchen. I didn't look at Gideon. But to my surprise, I didn't feel terrified of him. I felt angry. Really angry. Which didn't make any sense at all. He hadn't done anything to me.

I was choking my way through dinner, not tasting a thing, barely able to concentrate on the conversation. My mother was talking about Mimi, as usual. "I think she started to practice some Jewish rituals before she died. When I was going through her things, I found Sabbath candles and a menorah. Maybe when you get to a certain age you start thinking about your childhood more, and things that didn't seem that important suddenly do. I guess that's why she wanted all of us to experience a traditional Passover seder with her."

I was thinking that if Mimi hadn't found religion, she'd still be alive, but my mother said, "I'm glad she could reconnect with her past, even if it was for a short time."

"Is that why you said prayers before dinner tonight?" Gideon asked.

"In a way. I'm not connecting with my own childhood, but I'm connecting with ancient traditions I've grown to love," my mother answered. She looked at me. "And respect," she added.

Ordinarily I would have mouthed off at this point, bringing up some of the rituals in the Bible that aren't all that terrific. But I decided to let it go. Then suddenly I realized I'd lost track of the conversation, and everyone was talking politics.

"I think most families who have lost someone want peace," my father said.

I wanted revenge. I wanted to see every terrorist crushed.

"I don't hate the Palestinians," Shoshanna said. "There's enough hatred on both sides, and we need to find a way to stop it."

I couldn't believe she was saying this. How can you stop hatred?

"Why is it only the Jews who talk like that? Why are there thousands of us who stand at peace rallies? Why don't the Palestinians want peace?" I shouted. "They hate us! They want to destroy us. All of us." I could feel that my face was flushed with anger. Anger at everyone. Before I even knew what I was doing, I got up from the table, ran into my room, and slammed the door shut.

CHAPTER

32

After the anger passed, I felt humiliated, then upset with myself for allowing the anger to grab hold of me so unexpectedly. If anyone had the right to be angry, it was Shoshanna, not me. But things just seemed to be building up. Even though I thought I didn't care about anything, something was going on inside of me that I wasn't even aware of.

When I heard a knock on my door, I cringed, expecting my mother to open it and come in.

"Noa," Ari said, quietly.

If there was one person I was really embarrassed to see it was Ari. But if there was one person who wouldn't be upset with me for my outburst it was Ari.

"You can come in," I said.

He sat down on the bed beside me and didn't say anything for a while. I didn't say anything, either.

Finally, he started talking. "It's been a hard time for all of us. Mom and Dad and Shoshanna have battle scars to show what they experienced. I was in prison. But I think we sometimes forget that you suffer, too."

"Me? Why me?! I wasn't there when the dining room blew up. I was at Mimi's, talking on the phone!"

He looked at me for a moment, taking in what I'd just told him. I'd never said it out loud before. It felt strangely liberating but somehow binding. I wondered what Ari would think of me, now that he knew the truth.

"This friend of mine—this soldier—Joel—was driving back to base with his best buddy. He wanted to get something to eat. His buddy said they didn't really have time, but Joel persuaded him to stop for some pizza, anyway."

"I don't want to hear it. I know what you're going to say. It has nothing to do with me."

"Just hear me out."

I turned away from him and silently counted the number of tiles on the floor.

"Of course, you know what happened. Joel's buddy was killed. He didn't know it at the time. The last thing he remembers is looking over at his buddy and seeing him lying beside him in the pizza parlor, totally intact. He thought he'd just passed out. Joel suffered some minor injuries and was taken to the hospital. He asked his parents about his buddy, and they told him he was in the hospital, too. But the next day Joel picked up a newspaper, and there was his buddy's picture. That's how he found out about his buddy's death."

"So, lucky him. He survived."

"Yeah, he was lucky he survived, but because it was his idea to stop for pizza he feels like he killed his buddy."

"That's ridiculous," I said, quickly.

"I know," my brother said. "But he's in pain, anyway, even though he was barely touched."

"He didn't kill his buddy. Why don't you just tell him that?"

"I've tried."

"Well, then, tell him the suicide bomber killed his buddy. That's who he should blame, not himself," I said, exasperated.

"You're right. That's exactly what I should say," Ari said, and he took my hand, just the way he'd taken Shoshanna's when she was in the hospital.

I felt like crying—something I hadn't done for a long time—so I looked away from him again and concentrated on the pictures hanging on my wall. On my side of the room are the photographs I took two summers ago of cactuses in the desert. I like the way they look when they're in bloom. Flowers and prickles. If you get too close, you can get hurt.

I kept looking at the photographs. Pretty soon my breathing was shallow, and I bit my bottom lip, trying to call up the anger again because it was easier to tolerate than the hurt.

"The suicide bomber killed Mimi and maimed Shoshanna, Noa. You don't have to blame yourself for not getting there in time to be blown up, too."

"How can you say that to me?" I yelled, yanking my hand away from him.

"Because you gave me permission."

"I should have been there," I said, more softly. "The phone call was for Shoshanna. Gideon called *her.*"

I couldn't go on.

"Is that why you're so angry with Gideon?"

"I'm not angry with him."

"Could have fooled me. You trying to fool yourself?"

"I was flirting with him on the phone. I was acting like a complete idiot. He thinks I'm a kid. He shouldn't have just kept talking to me, like he was interested in me," I blurted out.

"Well, I'm sure he is interested in you. You're a very interesting person."

"Oh yeah. Right."

"Gideon feels guilty, too, Noa."

I couldn't believe what I was hearing. Why should Gideon feel guilty?

"He feels guilty because he can still play the cello, and Shoshanna can't play her violin."

"Well, that's really stupid. If everyone stopped their lives because a friend got hurt, the whole country would come to a standstill."

"Like you did?"

"What do you mean?"

"Mom told me about your grades. About dropping out of debate class. About not running."

I shrugged. "I just didn't care. They didn't seem worth caring about."

"Maybe if you cared about one thing, you'd have to care about other things, too."

I didn't dispute what he was saying because I didn't understand it entirely.

"I felt guilty, too," Ari said. "I was safe in prison and not at the hotel to protect my family. Isn't that what soldiers are supposed to do? Protect people? I couldn't even protect the people I love."

I looked at Ari for a long time, and somehow his words were reflected in a mirror hidden way down inside of me. I took a deep breath and let it out, and I realized that this was the first time I'd really breathed since the incident. Until now, I'd thought it was because of the smoke. The smoke and the smell of burning flesh. Until this minute, I'd thought I was trying to keep myself from inhaling those smells into my memory.

"After I saw Shoshanna, after I got back to base, I was a wreck. Shaking all over most of the time. This morning, Dr. Fried helped me figure out why."

"That idiot," I said automatically, but without much conviction.

"He's a little stiff, but he's not really an idiot. Why don't you try talking to him?"

"Because I really don't want to. If I had wanted to talk to anyone, I would have talked to Ronit—the counselor at school."

"Then talk to me. I've known you all your life, grasshopper. I told you how I felt—still feel sometimes when the guilt catches me off guard."

"I feel—I feel—I feel so frustrated! I just want to lash out at someone! The terrorists hurt all of us. I hate them!"

"So because you don't know any terrorists, you lash out at the people you love," Ari said, teasing me just enough to open me up, rather than shut me down again.

All of the tears I'd been holding in came flooding out. I fell back on my bed and cried.

"No wonder you like those cactuses so much," Ari said, after I stopped. "You're just like them. A real sabra. Prickly on the outside and sweet on the inside."

CHAPTER
33

I had fallen asleep. I guess the crying must have worn me out. When I opened my eyes, the room was completely dark. Ari had covered me and left. He was probably asleep in his own room. I looked at the clock. It was 2:30 a.m. For the first time since Passover, I had had a dreamless sleep. I looked over at Shoshanna's bed and was surprised to see it hadn't been slept in.

I staggered out of bed, famished.

As I headed down the hallway toward the kitchen, carefully avoiding knocking against the walls, I heard people talking quietly in the living room. And I could smell something burning. I gasped as memories flooded my senses. Then I realized it was only the smell of wood burning in the fireplace. Though the days were very warm, the nights were really cold. I shivered and was about to turn back to my room. I didn't want to see anyone or talk to anyone just then. But I heard the voices more clearly. Shoshanna and Gideon were talking.

I crept closer to the doorway, hoping no one would catch me eavesdropping. I hadn't meant to do it, but I was too curious to turn back.

I heard Shoshanna laugh quietly, and I was surprised. I hadn't heard her laugh like that in months. I wondered if I'd missed something, if I'd been seeing her world through my own lens and not through hers.

"All those days in the hospital I lay there silently raging at the world," I heard her tell him. "I felt as if my life had been taken away from me and just the shell was left. I couldn't image myself without my music. That was my complete identity. It had been from the time I was eight years old."

"But you went to school, had friends, traveled, did lots of things," Gideon whispered to her.

"I did all those things, but I did them as if I were half awake. The only time I was really alive was when I was playing the violin. "

"I don't feel that way," Gideon said. "Maybe that's why I'm not as great a musician as you are. As you—" He cleared his throat.

"It's okay," she said. "You can say it. As I was."

"Shoshanna," he said, his voice cracking with tenderness.

Thirty-three

"I'm not going to tell you that I'm glad it happened," she said. "That would be a lie. But, in a certain way, I'm glad I have the chance to find out who I am. It's kind of strange, really. These past few months I've realized that the emptiness I've felt isn't just because I can't play music."

"I've missed you so much."

"You missed the old me," she said, with a laugh. "This is the new me. I guess you'll have to get used to it. I don't want to look at you and see pity in your eyes. If that's what I see, then I won't want you to come around."

I was taken aback. I had no idea Shoshanna was so strong.

"That's not pity you see," Gideon mumbled.

I heard rustling noises, then a sigh.

"I never even had time for a boyfriend."

"You do now."

I heard what sounded like kissing, and I slid down to the floor.

I sat there for a while before tip-toeing back to my room. Then I slowly let out a sigh of relief. I really didn't have a crush on Gideon any more. He had no interest in running or horseback riding. We didn't actually have that much in common. I smiled. And that last bit of anger I felt toward him faded away.

CHAPTER
34

I didn't wake up until after ten. As soon as I opened my eyes, I wondered if what I'd heard the night before had been a dream. I looked over at Shoshanna's bed, and she was still sleeping. So I slipped quietly out of the room.

When I entered the kitchen, I heard sounds coming from my father's workshop and saw my mother's coffee cup in the sink. She'd already left for Sabbath services, I was sure.

I stepped outside onto the patio. The sun was beating down so hard it felt like a punishment. Squinting to shield my eyes, I could see Ari in the distance, hiking away from the house.

My whole body felt dry and itchy, so I went back inside. Automatically, I walked to the phone.

"Sarah?" I said, almost surprised at myself for calling her. Usually I waited for her to call me. I was her regular charity case. Even when I ignored her, which I usually did, she stopped by or at least called to say hi.

"Yeah," she said, nervously. I knew she wasn't sure if I was going to invite her over or yell at her for some minor infraction.

"It's so hot."

"Must be *hamsin*."

"Must be," I said. "It's already scorching. The winds are so dry, my hair's straight. Want to go to the pool?"

She didn't answer for a moment.

"While it's still daylight?"

"I—you haven't been to the pool all summer."

"And?"

"And nothing. I'm just surprised you want to go, that's all. I've only asked you about a hundred times."

"So now I'm asking you."

"Okay."

"Well, that was enthusiastic."

"Noa—"

"Yeah?"

126

"I told Matti I'd meet him at the pool today. He's working over at the stables every morning, then—"

"Matti?"

"I told you we were friends."

"Friends?"

"Friends."

Just as I thought. Everyone had abandoned me. My mother was at services. My father had been working away on some project for months, and he was too busy to do anything else. My brother was hiking. My sister was probably dreaming about Gideon. Even my best friend was hanging out with my backup boyfriend.

"Okay, so never mind," I said, feeling very sorry for myself.

"Matti will be glad to see you. I'll be over in an hour."

Before I could back out, she hung up the phone. And though I didn't want to admit it to myself, I was glad. My conversation with Ari had changed the way I felt. But it wasn't so easy to change the way I acted. Maybe Ari was right. Maybe there were things I really didn't understand about myself. Two minutes after I had called Sarah, I had been nasty to her for no reason at all. In the pit of my stomach, I still felt angry. Maybe I shoved down other feelings, too. Maybe I shoved them down so deeply I didn't even know they existed.

I picked up my mother's phone book and looked for Dr. Fried's phone number. "You have reached the office of Dr. Moshe Fried," the machine said. Just as I was about to hang up, I heard, "Hello."

"This is—Noa," I said, tentatively.

"Noa, what a lucky thing you called just now. I'm between clients, but I have a cancellation at one o'clock. Why don't you come in if you're free?"

"Well, I didn't say that I wanted to come in."

"Oh. Is everything all right, then?"

"Sure."

"Well, then, it was nice talking with you."

"Wait!"

"I'm sorry, but someone's just come into my outer office, Noa. I'm going to have to say good-bye, but—"

"I'll see if either my father or Ari can drive me," I said, quickly.

"I'll assume that you're coming," he said and hung up.

I just stood there, furious. How dare he just assume I was coming in? Like he'd known all along that I would eventually call him? Forget it, I thought. I didn't really want to talk to him anyway. I'd wait until school started again and talk to Ronit.

Then some little voice inside of me told me to calm down. I knew why I didn't want to see Dr. Fried. I was scared. Sure, I'd sat in his office for months, but I hadn't participated much in the sessions. I hadn't let myself, and while the rest of my family had moved on, in their ways, I was still angry and sad. I thought my talk with Ari had cured me, that that would be enough, but it obviously was just a beginning.

My father said he would be happy to drop me off at Dr. Fried's office, so I called Sarah and told her that I was sorry I had been so cranky. I was going to lie and say that I had forgotten that I had an appointment, so I would have to cancel our plans, but instead I found myself telling her the truth. She understood. I guess I knew she would.

Even though I had called him, I wasn't overjoyed to see Dr. Fried. I still didn't like him all that much, and in my head I still referred to him as Dr. Freud or even Dr. Fraud, but I thought I might learn something, anyway. We started off pretty badly, though. I had expected him to be as gentle with me as he had been with the rest of my family, but he wasn't. Well, maybe because I had been looking for an argument from the moment I walked into his office. Finally, he asked me why I was trying so hard to push him away. I just sat there, stunned. That was exactly what I had been doing. It was exactly what I had been doing with everyone in my life.

Suddenly, I started to cry. Again! I thought I had gotten out all of my tears the night before. I was totally mortified, but Dr. Fried leaned over and handed me a tissue. He just kept nodding, as if he understood why I was crying, even though I didn't. But I just kept crying anyway.

We didn't resolve everything in that session. Or in the next four or five, but by the time I walked out of Dr. Fried's office that day, I understood that I had abandoned my family and my friends because, on some deep level, I was afraid they would abandon me—just as Mimi had. So I had abandoned them first. I knew rationally that Mimi hadn't chosen to abandon me; but I had come to grips with that only in my head, and not in my heart. It took the rest of the summer to understand how that had affected my life, and it took longer than that to allow myself to feel my losses, though there was one major loss that I wasn't ready to address until much later.

When I got back from Dr. Fried's office, it was only 2:30. I had the rest of the day ahead of me. I was feeling pretty emotional as I walked toward my bedroom: liberated in a way, sad because of everything we'd discussed, and relieved because I felt that we would eventually be able to excavate all those dark shadows that lurked deep inside of me. And hopefully with some help I would be able to face them and defeat them. I knew—at least, I was beginning to know—that people really did care about me.

So when I decided it was time to come out of my shell and attempt to reconnect with the world, I changed into my bathing suit and walked over to the swimming pool. I knew reentry wouldn't be easy. It never is. But Mr. Drucker was right. We have choices.

Matti felt awkward, and I felt awkward. We hadn't really talked to each other since I blew him off my first day back at school after Mimi's funeral. But Sarah was being Sarah—happy we were all together. There were no secret looks between us, signifying that she knew that I had just seen Dr. Fried, and that I knew that she knew. I just wanted them to know that I had changed, and I guess my being there was their first clue. I'm not going to tell you that it was easy; it wasn't. Change is never easy. But sometimes it's necessary. And sometimes you have to tell yourself to concentrate on your goal and just go for it.

One of the advantages of living in Beit Zeit is the Olympic-sized swimming pool. That day it was really crowded, and I was barely able to squeeze in between Sarah and two other teenagers. A woman and her kids were squeezed next to Matti. She was yelling at them in Spanish.

Sarah and Matti had already been in the water, but I was boiling, so we walked down the steps from the upper tier and plunged into the cold water. You could barely swim a foot without bumping into little kids playing Marco Polo, but that was okay. I didn't mind all that much.

When we went back to our towels, we didn't even bother drying off. The hot winds did it for us.

"Heard the news today?" Matti asked.

I suddenly realized that, for the first time I could remember, I hadn't heard the news. I hadn't even thought about turning on the radio that morning.

Sarah glanced at me. Then she gave Matti a look.

"So, come down to the stables, Noa," Matti said. "Since I'm working there, I can cut you a deal. You can ride for half price."

"What was on the news, Matti?" I asked.

"Nothing much. Nothing different."

"What?"

"Let's just have one day without talking politics," Sarah said.

"Did you ever think what your life would be like if you were a Palestinian?" I asked as I rolled over on my towel. I looked at the dry grass, flicked away some stones, thought about Maha for a moment, then pushed the thought away.

"Not really," Sarah said. "It's hard enough being an Israeli."

We all laughed.

"If you weren't an Israeli, what would you like to be?" Matti asked.

"A race horse," I said, without hesitation.

"Come on. You know what I mean. Anyway, with your luck, you'd wind up with foot-and-mouth disease. Whatever that is."

"What do you mean—with my luck?" I said, laughing. "Everyone always tells me I'm lucky. I *am* lucky."

"She is lucky," Sarah said. "She should have failed chemistry instead of getting a 3. She didn't even bother taking the final."

"And anyway, I'm more likely to wind up with foot-*in*-mouth disease," I added.

"Yeah. Yeah. Yeah," Matti said. "The baddest mouth in the West. West Jerusalem."

"I'm also the fastest mouth," I said, jumping up. I threw my sunglasses down on my towel. "Last one to swim from the shallow end to the deep end downloads the new Justin Timberlake CD."

I yanked Sarah up and pushed her toward the steps before Matti had a chance to get his sunglasses off.

Racing toward the pool, I laughed out loud. I jumped in and swam around in what seemed like circles as I tried to avoid the kids playing Marco Polo. I didn't even notice that Matti and Sarah had already reached the other end of the pool. They were waving their arms at me in triumph. But I didn't care. I just kept swimming toward the deep end. Happy to be with them. Happy to be alive.

CHAPTER

35

So what began as my summer of discontent evolved into a summer of self-knowledge. Some people call it growing up. I prefer to say that Dr. Fried helped me learn how to listen to my own voice, the one deep inside. Sarah and Matti and I formed a unified front, daring the world to say NO to our YES.

But there was still an unresolved issue that I had never discussed with Dr. Fried, or with anyone. Sometimes when I least expected it, it nagged at me. I'd see a Palestinian woman on the street and think of Maha, or I would hear something funny and know that she would laugh if I repeated it to her. Or I would lie in bed at night and yearn to call her, to hear her voice, to let her know that I missed her, but then I'd tell myself that it was too late. And I would push down my feeling and think about something else.

So senior year began, and Sara and Matti and I studied together. My grades were back up, and Sarah decided she could do advanced chemistry as well as I. I agreed. I also finally realized that if I stopped insisting that everything had to be as concrete as math, I could understand the layers of meaning in poetry.

My father and Abed had reconnected a few months before, just like Sarah and me. Only they had never really argued. It was more like an embarrassment between them after the massacre. Then they met by accident one day, and they decided to sit down for coffee. By the end of the hour, my father had agreed to meet with a group of Palestinians and Israelis who had lost family members during the intifada. Abed told my father about a Palestinian man whose son was killed by an Israeli soldier. Of course, the man was angry and hurt, but one day an Israeli knocked on his door and said he was so sorry for his loss, that he knew what the Palestinian man was feeling because he had suffered the same loss. The Israeli started to cry. It was the first time the Palestinian had spoken to an Israeli who wasn't holding a gun.

I felt strange, at first, seeing Abed in our house again. I couldn't look at him. I knew he could feel that. He had felt it the day of Mimi's funeral, when I didn't even know I felt it. So, when he mentioned that he had seen Maha at a family party, and that she had asked about me, I felt it was a kind of a test. And I also knew that in order to pass the test, I would have to call her.

At the end of September, even though I was pretty scared, and even though it would have been easier to keep pretending that I wasn't sad about the loss of our friendship, I finally made the call. I didn't know if Maha was still interested in talking to me, or if she even remembered how close we had been. We had an awkward conversation, but we agreed to meet on neutral territory at a café near the Old City.

On the way there, I thought about the times we had met before and the times we had spoken on the phone. Sometime during my visit to her house, we had each begun to let down our guard, and during the phone calls that followed, we had begun to establish a friendship. When I had called her because I had been so upset with Mimi, she had understood in a way no one else could have. She had been a good friend. And we had a lot in common. We liked the same music, especially old Beatles songs. We were both runners, both liked math and chemistry. We even talked about guys. We had begun relating to each other as just girls—not as an Israeli and a Palestinian. Until last Passover.

As I sat on the bus, I couldn't stop myself from thinking that she had invited me to Abu Dis all those months ago because she had had some kind of agenda, something to prove. We hadn't actually argued that day at the bus stop, but we had certainly lobbed a few political bricks at each other, so I was surprised that she had tracked me down then. And I was surprised that she wanted to meet me again after the way I had treated her. The question was why. Why did she still want me for a friend?

Abed had said that Maha was lonely. Most of her old friends had dropped her when she decided to attend Hebrew University. But she'd heard all the nightmarish stories about students waiting for hours to cross the checkpoints from the Israeli side of Abu Dis to the Palestinian side in order to get to classes at Al Quds, the Palestinian university. And she decided there were just too many barriers. The regulations about who could cross and who couldn't seemed to change almost every day, so even though she felt isolated at Hebrew University, she knew she would be able to get there, at least most of the time. But I wasn't sure if I wanted to be her friend just because she was lonely.

Maha was waiting for me when I got off the bus. For a moment, I was afraid that I wouldn't recognize her. It had been a long time. But she waved to me as I walked toward her. It was a half wave, as if she weren't quite sure how to greet me.

We sat down and ordered coffees that got cold as we tried to find the right words to reconnect.

"My father sent this for you," she said, as she slid a slender book across the table.

Thirty-five

"Propaganda?" I asked, trying to make a joke, which really wasn't funny. I immediately regretted it.

Maha stood up and snatched the book back. "Not unless you consider poetry propaganda. Call me when you're ready to be a friend. Or better yet—don't call me till you learn how to be a friend."

"I'm sorry."

Maha started walking away as if she hadn't heard me.

"Maha," I said, getting up. I reached for her arm. "I don't know why I said that."

She yanked her arm away.

"You're right. Sometimes I don't know how to be a friend."

"How can I trust you when you say such hurtful things?"

"I don't know," I answered, honestly. "But if the two of us can't trust each other, I have to wonder how your people and my people are ever going to find a common ground."

Suddenly, she started to giggle. Giggle! I looked at her as if she had lost her mind. What was she laughing about? She just kept on giggling until tears started streaming out of her eyes.

"Common ground," she said between giggles. "That's the whole problem, isn't it? You say it's your ground, and we say it's our ground."

"It's just a stupid cliché—a metaphor," I said, but I started laughing, too. "I didn't mean it literally."

"I know. I know," she said. "That's what makes it so funny."

"You say it's yours, and I say it's mine. I say it's yours, and you say it's mine. I don't know why you say it's yours; I say it's mine," I sang to the tune of the Beatles' song "Hello Goodbye."

Smiling, we both sat down again.

"Maybe some day it'll be different," I said.

"It will be," she said.

I wasn't sure what she meant by that, but I was determined to let it be. Instead of chancing another argument, I started talking about music. What was hot and what wasn't. Then we talked about movies. We both love French and American films. She thinks French films are better. I like American films better, so we had a friendly argument, both of us careful to stay within the proscribed boundaries.

After spending the afternoon together, we understood that possibilities for a real friendship existed, but I think we both knew that we might have to continue facing our demons instead of running away from them. We had found a common language, but neither of us felt completely comfortable with the other. After our first little "misunderstanding," we were too polite, which probably should have been a clue that both of us were holding back. I know I was. Sure, I had pretty much stopped hating all Palestinians for what a few dozen had done, but some days, like that day, things just slipped out of my mouth, and I still looked for terrorists around every corner. And truthfully, if Maha hadn't been related to Abed, I'm not so sure I would have finally returned her calls. But I was glad I had, and before we left the table, she slipped the poetry book into my purse.

Still, I felt that Abed was holding back something vital, and so was she. But we all pretended that even though both the Israelis and the Palestinians were killing each other daily, we were above it all. We were able to see beyond all the labels. In the end, it took a shock for us to totally let down our guards.

CHAPTER
36

The year sped by, and then it was Passover again. Exactly one year since the Passover Massacre, since Mimi had been killed, since Shoshanna had played the violin. At sundown, before we began our seder, my mother lit a special candle for Mimi to commemorate the anniversary of her death.

There were many beginnings and endings to think about that night of our seder. For one thing, it was the end of a year of mourning for Mimi—and for all the other victims of the Passover Massacre. That didn't mean we would forget Mimi, only that we could begin to let go of the sorrow and remember the ways in which she was still part of us. And because Ari had been discharged from the army on grounds of so-called unsuitability, he could share in our healing, as well. He had begun working with the high school graduates who had refused to sign up for the draft. It was also the end of winter and the beginning of spring. Everything was starting to bloom, including my sister. Shoshanna and Gideon had just begun their life together. After the seder they would go back to the apartment they'd rented in the city.

We had all been nervous about Passover, dreading it actually. But we decided that it would be a good idea to share this Passover with Abed and Dahlia. And Abed suggested that we invite Maha, as well. He would be happy to pick her up, he said. So there we were, sitting around the seder table: my mother, my father, Ari, Shoshanna, Gideon, Abed, Dahlia, Maha, and me.

The table held a platter of spring vegetables, and a vase filled with blood red chrysanthemums flanked the seder plate. Mimi's favorite vase held the flowers. That year, for the first time, my mother conducted a service. Naturally, we'd studied Exodus in school and learned about Moses bringing the Israelites out of Egypt. But reading the story in the haggadah put another spin on it.

As my mother continued, I realized that one by one we each became aware that this seder, in a way, replaced the seder we had never gotten to attend. My mother read the part in the haggadah about the four sons, one wise, one contrary, one who is simple, and one who doesn't even know how to ask a question. I squirmed a little when she mentioned the contrary son who asks, "What is the meaning of this service to you?"

Toward the middle of the service my mother put down the haggadah and looked at us. "Okay, so we've just read about the exodus of the Jewish people from Egypt, where they were slaves under the Pharaoh. We all know that the story took place thousands of years ago, but I was wondering why it might still be relevant today—aside from the tradition of our retelling it."

"I guess we're all slaves to something," Ari said.

"Exactly," my mother agreed.

Oh no. Here comes the third grade teacher in her, I thought. She was shifting into classroom gear. "I'm a slave to hunger," I said. "Can't we just get to the food part of the seder and skip the relevant thing?"

"Give it a rest, contrary daughter," Shoshanna said to me.

Gideon caught my eye and smiled.

"Okay. Okay."

"Maybe I could start," Abed said, quietly. "I think I've been a slave to the image of myself as a white knight. Given my dark skin, I should have known it was just an illusion," he added with a little laugh. "But there you are; I bought into it, anyway. And I've surrounded myself with plenty of things to convince me of that illusion. My horse. Every knight needs a horse. Being a doctor, so I could heal the sick. What I realized, as I listened to this service, is that I'm like the son who didn't even know how to ask a question. Caught up in my own image, sometimes I forget to ask myself who I really am."

"I know who you are," Maha said, vehemently. "You may not be a white knight, but you're a hero to our people."

"And I know who you are," Dahlia said, as she gently touched Abed's arm. "That's why I love you. But I'm a slave, as well. I'm a slave to biology." She looked at my mother. "All these years I've been a dutiful daughter. I've lived alone because my mother said she'd die if I married Abed. But now I'm forty years old. My biological clock is ticking. I want to have a child."

She stopped talking, and we sat there on edge. Abed was holding his breath as she turned back to him.

"If you still want to marry me, I say yes," she said. A radiant smile spread across her face, so that all I could see were red lips pressed against white teeth. "My mother won't die, but I may if I continue to be a slave to her wishes."

We all started to clap, and Abed clasped Dahlia's hand. Then he kissed it. It was so incredibly romantic, I was sure, at that moment, that his being a white knight was no illusion.

"Well, it looks like it wasn't such a bad idea to make our seder more personal," my mother said, grinning.

136

And that was true.

"Who wants to go next?" she said, looking around the table.

Nobody said anything for a moment. Then Shoshanna started speaking softly. "I'm a slave to my ego," she said. "I felt that if I couldn't be the best violinist, I didn't want to play at all, but I've begun to practice in secret. If you're ready for a brief concert to celebrate Abed and Dahlia's engagement, I'll show you what I can do."

Everyone except my father was amazed. We all started talking at once, unable to understand how she could even hold the bow in her hand, let alone play. But Shoshanna wouldn't answer any of our questions. Instead she got her violin, and my father helped her snap on a device he had fashioned for her to allow her fingers to hold the bow.

With everything in place, she began playing, "Had Gadya," a simple Passover song. It wasn't Brahms, but we were all listening intently, as if her playing was some kind of miracle. When she finished, her faced was flushed. We gave her a standing ovation, and she bowed, almost as pleased, it seemed, as when she had bowed before an audience of thousands.

I didn't think anyone could top that for emotion. It would have been so easy for Shoshanna to give up playing the violin. She had everyone's sympathy for her loss. What a great story—if it isn't *your* life.

"My sister is much braver than I am," Ari said. "In her imagination, she still hears the music she used to make. In her dreams, she holds her bow, gliding it across the strings like a ballet dancer pirouetting across the floor. But tonight she was willing to be less than perfect. And we were all moved by that. Me? I'm a slave to perfection. Since sixth grade I've been writing stories."

We all looked at him as if he were making this up at the spur of the moment.

"Yeah, I know," he said, and he laughed softly. "You're probably wondering where all these stories are. I burn them in the fireplace or stuff them into the garbage can after I tear them into tiny shreds."

"Ari," my mother groaned, as if she couldn't bear to hear him go on.

"After I was drafted, I stopped writing. The stories have formed in my head, but I have been afraid to write them down. I've been afraid they won't be perfect. But tonight—tonight I've learned something. None of us is perfect."

He glanced at the table for a moment. "I look at all these symbols on the seder plate: the egg, the lamb bone, the bitter herbs, the *haroset*, the parsley. The bitter and the sweet. Hope where there didn't seem to be any. But, you know what? Exodus isn't only about Moses leading the Jews out of bondage. It's also about being a stranger in a strange land. And I'm wondering how we can celebrate our own liberation when we sometimes treat the so-called strangers in our land like slaves. I want to write about that," Ari said, softly. "And I want people to read it."

"That was very beautiful, Ari," said Abed.

"And moving," Dahlia agreed.

"But who are the *real* strangers?" Maha asked.

Dahlia looked at Abed. She didn't say anything for a moment. Then she began speaking slowly. "I must tell you that as much as I hope for freedom for the Palestinians, I really don't know if peace is possible. There's so much anger. On both sides." She glanced at Maha. "Many Palestinians think this is an Arab part of the world."

"My family lives in a house once owned by an Arab family," Gideon said, quietly. "And yes, I think about that sometimes. But life goes on. The world changes, and we have to change with it or be left behind."

Maha had willed her face to remain expressionless, but her eyes were flashing signals to Abed.

"But Dahlia's right. There are Arabs—not only Arabs—who believe that it's unnatural for us Jews to live here. That we don't belong," Ari countered. "And sometimes—sometimes—I think maybe they're right."

"Ari—" Abed cautioned.

"Where do we belong?" my mother pleaded.

My throat got tight. As much as I complained about Israel, as much as I hated living in fear, it was the only country I knew. The thought of having to leave it forever terrified me.

"We belong where we are," my father said. "This is the only home I know. We're here now, regardless of how we got here. We're here to stay."

"Of course you are" Abed said, automatically. "I don't agree with Ari. You belong here as much as I do." He hesitated for a moment before going on. Then it looked as if he had suddenly been stricken by some phantom pain. "But even as I say that—and even though I believe it—some part of me feels that what Ari said is true. I think deep down in my heart, I feel that this land was stolen from my people."

"It was," Maha said, quietly. "It was," she repeated, glaring at Gideon.

Oh no, I almost said aloud. It was okay for Maha and me to spar in private, but it wasn't okay to fight in public.

"You try to convince everyone that there was no such country as Palestine. As if we were all just nomads in the desert, and that it took you Israelis to make the desert bloom. Go outside. Look at the ancient olive trees in your backyard. Who do you think planted them in the first place?" she asked.

"And who dug the wells that the Israeli army destroys so that the refugees driven off their land—which is now your land—have no water to drink?" Abed asked.

I sneaked a glance at Dahlia as Abed continued speaking. Dahlia's jaw was tightly clenched. She turned away from him, as if looking at him kept her from the challenge of her own thoughts.

"I want it to end—this terrible war, this awful loss of innocent lives on both sides," Abed continued. He tried to take Dahlia's hand. She grasped her fork more tightly. "But in all honesty," he said, "if I could will the Israelis away without bloodshed, I would."

"How can you talk like that?" Dahlia cried. She freed her hand from Abed's and gripped the sides of her chair. "You're saying that if you could make me disappear, you would."

"Not you, Dahlia!"

"Not me? Who then? David? Lilah? The children?"

"We lived together peacefully—before the country was divided. Before there was a Jewish state," Maha said, not quite understanding why we refused to accept what was so obvious to her.

"You were welcome in Palestine," Abed continued. "But your people became greedy. Palestine will ultimately be a Muslim country again. It may not happen next year or in ten years, but it will happen. And your people will be welcome again."

"Greedy!? You've crossed the line, Abed," Dahlia said, angrily.

The rest of us at the table didn't know what to do with ourselves. My mother got up, saying it was time for the main course. I jumped up to help her, relieved to turn my back on Abed and Dahlia. And on Maha. But the tension in the room imprisoned me, and I was unable to move from where I stood.

Slumped down in his chair, my father looked crushed. "Abed," he started to say. But Dahlia interrupted him. She threw her napkin on the table and glared at Abed.

"I don't really know you. I've been with you for fifteen years, and I don't even know you," she said.

"Don't be angry with me, Dahlia. I want peace as much as you do, but—"

"But you'd be just as happy if we all fell into the sea."

Her hands shaking, my mother carried a platter of chicken into the room. I like drama. Sometimes I even like to create it myself, but this drama was so sad and unsettling, I wished they'd both disappear into the sea and take Maha with them.

"You're just like Yasir Arafat," Dahlia spat out. "Excuse me," she said, getting up. "I'm sorry we ruined your beautiful seder."

"I'm sorry you ruined it," Abed said, angrily. He got up, as well. "I don't like being compared to Yasir Arafat."

"Then stop acting like him."

"Good night, Lilah, David," Abed said, curtly. He walked out of the house, leaving Dahlia standing there.

The air in the room was tense with her anger and our embarrassment. The light drained out of her face, and she looked like someone who had lost a game in which the rules had changed.

"I feel totally betrayed," Dahlia said, quietly. "I put all my cards on the table, and he walked out."

We were all looking at Dahlia, so nobody noticed that Maha had stood up, as well. "That day when we got off the bus," she said to me, "I was so angry with you." She was speaking quietly, but that only made what she had to say more difficult to hear. "How easy it was for you to almost ruin someone else's life."

"It was a misunderstanding," I said, trying lamely to defend myself.

"Misunderstandings can be lethal," she said, and I could tell that even though she kept her voice low, she was seething. Her hands were shaking. I blinked, not sure exactly what she meant, but she suddenly turned to Gideon.
"You," she said, "you live in the house of my cousin or my cousin's cousin or maybe not a relative at all, but someone who misunderstood the signals and ran because he was afraid the Jews would slaughter him. Now my cousin or my cousin's cousin can't come home. Ever, as far as you're concerned, because you live in his house, and the government won't let him back into the country. His country. Our country."

Gideon shook his head. "I know. I understand what you're saying, and I'm sure I would feel the same way if I were you."

"But you're not, so you have the luxury of living in what could have been my house while we're forced to live with strangers."

"But you live in Abu Dis," I said, confused.

"And my grandparents and aunts and uncles lived in Ramallah, but their houses were ransacked by Israeli soldiers after what happened in Netanya. They were terrified. They left the country. We couldn't even get to them because of the roadblock."

Her words were spilling out now, one after the other, as if she couldn't stop them. "But even before that, my brother was arrested for something he didn't do. So he's gone, too," she said, finally vomiting up the secret she'd kept from me.

My mouth dropped open. "You never told me that. Abed never told me—us—any of us."

"I asked him not to. It changes the whole dynamic. I wanted you to know me first. Me. Maha. Not me the victim."

Maha's eyes were flashing now. She could barely contain her anger.

"I know what you mean," Shoshanna said.

"Yes, I'm sure you do," Maha said, more gently. "And I don't like what our terrorists do anymore than I like the work of your terrorists."

I could feel the anger welling up inside of me, and I started to say that our soldiers are not terrorists, that they only respond when they're provoked, that all we want is peace, and that if the terrorists would leave us alone, the Palestinians would never ever have to worry about us terrorizing them. We do not teach hatred in our schools. We don't tell our children that being a martyr for their country will bring them rewards in heaven. No Israeli mother would say what a Palestinian mother recently said—that the best Mother's Day present she got was the death of her son as a martyr. We do not blow ourselves up, killing innocent women and children. But before I could say anything, Ari spoke.

"Why was your brother arrested?" he asked.

Maha hesitated for a moment, as if telling her story somehow made it more real for her, as if she would have to relive it, as if she would have to feel the pain all over again. Finally, she began speaking slowly. "Some students from Al Quds were protesting, yelling that the wall and checkpoints kept them out of their own country, that Jerusalem is Arab, Muslim, and Christian. Israeli soldiers marched into Abu Dis and started firing rubber bullets. One of the protestors was shot in the face. Other students started hurling stones and fire bombs at the soldiers. A bunch of students were throwing stones at them from the rooftops of houses nearby. One of the kids hit a soldier in the eye with a stone from his sling shot."

She stopped talking and clenched her fist. We were riveted, waiting for her to continue. "Other soldiers started firing, and the kids jumped down from the roof and ran. One of them—my brother—ran smack into a soldier. He was terrified. He swore he had just been hanging out with his friends when the protest began. They had no intention of throwing any stones at anyone; then they spotted the soldiers, and one or two of the boys started hurling stones at them. My brother said he hadn't thrown one stone. He was completely innocent. He had no idea that his friends were going to pitch them at the soldiers."

We were all embarrassed by Maha's story. And I think she meant to embarrass us. Nobody knew what to say. Then suddenly Abed began speaking. None of us had noticed that he had walked back into the room.

"The soldiers came into Abu Dis because of the horrendous suicide bombing at the Sbarro Pizza restaurant in Jerusalem," he said. "The Israelis promised to retaliate, and they did by putting up barriers. Everyone was angry. The soldiers were angry because no Palestinian leader condemned the bombing. Instead one faction proudly took responsibility for it. The students were angry because their right to travel in what they consider their own country was once again taken away from them."

He turned to Maha. "If your brother and his friends hadn't been part of the protest, hadn't planned on attacking the soldiers, why had they hauled stones up to the roof? Why did they have their sling shots with them?" he asked, gently.

Maha put her hand over her mouth as if she wished she could take back her story. She and her family had done what most of us do. Tell that same story over and over again until it becomes the truth, never stopping to analyze it, never thinking it through. We react to our emotions. And just like Maha, every one of us was taken in by the reality of Maha's emotions and the guilt we all felt. It was only when Abed spoke up that we realized there was another side to the story.

"So, the question is: Who is David and who is Goliath? Shoshanna said to Maha. "It's an unanswerable question right now. That's why Ari refused to serve in the territories. He didn't want to be involved in one of those misunderstandings."
"The only way to avoid misunderstandings is to discuss them. War—any kind of war—isn't really a solution to anything," my father said. "But here in Israel we've begun to think that war is normal."

"But *both* sides have to agree to negotiate," my mother said, softly.

"Look," said Gideon, "I think the Palestinians should get back the occupied territories, but they and all of their allies—the Syrians, the Hezbollah terrorists in Lebanon, the Iranians—have to allow us to live in Israel without being afraid to walk into a pizza parlor. There can be no peace without justice. And there can be no justice unless both sides sit down and agree to honor specific boundaries. The Palestinians have to stop attacking our little piece of land."   Gideon looked directly at Abed, not really ready to allow him back into our conversation. "After all, look what happened to Goliath in the end."

Abed looked at Dahlia. I held my breath, afraid that he might say something else to hurt her, to hurt all of us. Instead, he gently put his hand on her hair. She stood there, looking tense and suddenly unsure of how to respond.

Finally Abed said, "Because we're all family, I hoped you'd understand my deepest feelings. Thoughts I hadn't really allowed myself to feel before. What you heard was my frustration speaking. Yes, there's truth to what I said. Life would be

142

much easier if this country were still simply Palestine. But it's not. Gideon was right. We can't live in the past. You're my friends, my dear friends."

He looked deeply into Dahlia's eyes. "And you're the woman I love." He turned toward the rest of us. "I don't want any of you to disappear from my life."

We all sat there, confused, stunned, and awkward. Then Abed caught my eye. We looked at each other, both of us acknowledging the pain and sorrow his confession and Maha's had caused. I could see the sadness in his eyes and the sadness in hers. And I almost started to cry. It's okay, I said with my eyes. We all have secrets we don't want to admit. We all hide things deep inside of us that can erupt, hurting the people we love. We all make mistakes. Even white knights in shining armor.

"It took a lot of courage for you to say something that was hard for us to hear," my father said.

The rest of us still remained silent. Then Dahlia sat back down, and Abed let out a deep breath and sat down next to her. We all knew there were lots of unsaid words between them and between Maha and me, words that would have to be said eventually. But for now—we were a family again.

"Shall we eat?" my mother asked as she began cutting up the chicken.

CHAPTER
37

This war has rained bullets of sadness and regret on all of us. The very air we breathe is filled with sorrow. Turn on the news, and what do we see? A suicide bombing. And after each suicide bombing, we hear about tanks rolling into the West Bank and Gaza. Soldiers killing and being killed. But the worst thing is the loss of hope that the situation will ever change.

I rolled over and got out of bed. Where is Moses when we need him?

"Mom," I called, as I walked into the kitchen, where she was putting away the dishes from the seder.

"You slept late," she said.

"I couldn't fall asleep last night."

"I guess I should have stuck to the haggadah," she said with a sigh.

"I'm glad you didn't," I said, as I opened the refrigerator and took out some fruit and yogurt.

"What do you have planned for the day?" she asked.

"Oh, I thought I'd meet Matti," I said, casually, as I dug into the yogurt.

"You and Matti more than just friends?" she asked, just as casually.

"Maybe."

"Hmmm. Interesting."

"Don't get all teary-eyed, Mom."

"I met your father when I was your age."

"Mom!"

"So what *are* you going to do?"

"I don't know. Maybe go horseback riding."

"Sounds good. Why don't you call Matti and set a time?"

"Why?" I asked, suddenly suspicious.

"No reason."

"Yes, reason. What are you planning, Mom?"

"I don't know why you think I'm planning anything."

"Look at you. You can't even answer my question."

My mother poured herself a cup of tea and sat down across from me. Running her finger along the side of the cup, she concentrated on the tea leaves as if they held the answers to all the whys of her existence. With her head bent, I noticed the gray, and it made me sad. Out of the corner of my eye, I studied her face. It looked as if someone had etched lines around her lips and in the corners of her eyes. I had never thought of my mother as old before. I had never thought of her as young, either. But looking at her at that moment, she seemed so vulnerable.

Maybe she's sick, I thought. In two minutes, I went from teasing her to complete panic. I started listing all the things I'd done to upset her—just in the last few days. Even though we didn't get along all of the time, I didn't want to lose her.

"I haven't told anyone else yet," she began cautiously. "But since Mimi died, I've been thinking. What I've finally realized is that it's hard to lose a father, too," she said.

I froze, unable to swallow the piece of orange I'd popped into my mouth.

"Last night I was going to say that every year when I get my father's birthday cards, I'm relieved that he's still thinking about me. Last Passover, as soon as he saw the list of fatalities, he called me. When I got his call, I was more than relieved; I was happy that he was still alive. And for the first time in over forty years, I could finally admit that I miss him. Admit that I've been hanging on to an anger I don't even feel any more."

"He called you. You talked to him? Why didn't you tell us?"

My mother reached over, took my hand, and squeezed it.

"Because I wasn't sure how I felt about him until last night. I wasn't sure that I wanted to bring him back into my life. After his first phone call, there were a few others. But it was one thing to talk on the phone, and another thing to think about actually seeing him again. Last night I was going to say that I was a slave to the past. I don't think I'd ever really forgiven my father for going back to Germany. But as I thought about what it would be like for me to move to another country, I realized why he had to leave Israel. Germany was his home."

"Lots of people come here from other places. Russia, Ethiopia, India, Italy, France, the United States. Why don't they want to go back?" I asked.

"Lots of them do go back. But those who stay, stay because this crazy country is home to them."

"I guess Germany was a pretty crazy country, too!"

"But that was where my father felt at home. He had come to Israel to right the wrongs his people had done to our people. He had loved me and my mother, but, in the end he felt like a stranger here."

"His people? Our people? What are you talking about?" I asked. Then I gasped. "You mean your father wasn't Jewish?"

"No. He wasn't. But it was never really discussed," my mother said. "Mimi just let it slip out one night, right before she died."

"You're kidding!"

"Sorry, I didn't mean to eavesdrop," Ari said.

My mom and I swung around in our chairs, surprised to see him standing in the doorway.

"Did you know about this?"

Ari shook his head. Then he came in, hugged my mother, and sat down next to her.

"Mom's half-German," I said, incredulous. I stared at my mother as if she had suddenly morphed into someone else. "I mean, I knew your father was German, but I never knew he was a German German." Suddenly, the incredible became inconceivable. "You mean, like a Nazi German? Was he a Nazi?"

"No," my mother said. "I had been afraid to ask him that question. But when he called yesterday morning to wish us a happy Passover, we finally had the conversation I think we've both been waiting to have."

Ari and I exchanged glances. This was unreal.

"My father was conscripted into the German army at seventeen, but he quickly deserted. After the war, he was part of a work force helping the Allies in a displaced person's camp. That's where he met Mimi—after the Americans had liberated Auschwitz, Mimi was taken to one of these camps. She weighed fifty pounds. My father nursed her back to health, and because he was so disgusted with the way his country had acted, he said he would help her get to Palestine. Which he did. But by that time, he was in love with her, so he stayed, learned Hebrew. Well, sort of. Then the State of Israel was declared, and I was born. He was happy, but he began feeling isolated. He's a writer. His language is German; there was no way for him to express himself here."

I could see how much my grandfather's story affected my mother. It affected me, too, picturing Mimi the way my mother had described her.

"Mimi wouldn't leave, of course. After what had happened to her, she wanted to feel safe, and she felt safe only in a Jewish country. My father became more and more miserable. Finally, he left. She never forgave him, though on some level, I think she must have understood."

My mother sat back in her chair for a moment; then she put her head in her hands and started to weep. I put my arms around her.

She sighed and looked out the glass door. Isaac, my land turtle, waddled up onto the patio and sluggishly made his way toward her.

"He promised Mimi that he wouldn't try to see me after he left, but I want to see him," she said, after a few minutes. "And I want him to see me. I'd like him to come here. I'd like him to meet my family. His family—"

She paused. "And if he won't come here, I'll go to him."

Still incredulous about my mother's announcement, I eventually wandered back toward my room. When I passed Ari's room, I heard him playing his guitar. I walked on. Then I turned back and stood in the doorway.

"Do you think it's true—what he told Mom?"

"Yeah. Otherwise, he probably wouldn't have married Mimi and brought her here."

"I'm glad he wasn't one of them—a Nazi."

"Me too. It's hard to understand the craziness that came over the Germans, but it seems as though people behave in extreme ways under extreme circumstances—as if they're propelled by a nightmare that's taken hold of their ability to reason. Maybe we're all susceptible to atrocious behavior under the right—or wrong—circumstances. Maybe I'm not such a hero for refusing to serve in the occupied territories. Maybe I just didn't want to test myself."

I heard what Ari was saying. On some level I understood it, but there was one thing I knew—regardless of the circumstances, Ari would never have treated another human being the way the Nazis had. As Mr. Drucker says, "People always have choices."

"When the band's playing, and everyone's shouting, 'Heil Hitler' or some other slogan, a certain sense of unreality grips people," Ari continued.

"Maybe."

"Like suicide bombers who have had the glories of martyrdom drummed into their heads. It's hard for us to believe they're really acting rationally. Maybe only people who are trained to question authority can stop the madness."

"Our grandfather wasn't trained to question authority, but he did. He tried to stop the madness."

"People have to be pretty exceptional to fight the system."

"Like you," I said.

"That's not what I meant," he said, blushing.

"Still, it's true."

"Because our grandfather didn't follow orders and stay in the German army, he saved Mimi's life."

My shoulders sank. "Which is more than I did," I mumbled.

"I thought we talked about that, Noa."

"There's one thing I didn't tell you about that night—"

Ari stopped playing and put his guitar down. He motioned for me to come into the room. I slumped down on his bed next to him.

"Mimi was really mad at me when she died. And I was really mad at her."

Ari looked at me for a long time. Then he smiled a little. "Mimi never stayed mad at any of us for long."

"I'm not talking about annoyed, Ari. I'm talking about anger. We were very, very angry at each other."

"Why?"

"When we were at Vered ha-Galil, we had a really bad argument, and she slapped me across the face."

Ari was as shocked by what I had said as I was the day it happened. He touched my face. "What were you arguing about?"

"About—" I stopped myself. "About politics," I said, finally.

"Yeah, she could get really upset about politics. I was afraid to tell her I was a refusenik. I suppose Mom did. Mimi was probably angry with me, too."

I looked at him for a long moment. "Mom never told her," I said. Then I leaned over and punched Ari in the arm. "Thanks."

"For what?"

"For listening. Maybe you're right. Maybe she wasn't angry at me anymore. But still, I never got to tell her that I loved her."

"I think she always knew that. You were her favorite, you know. You're just like her."

CHAPTER
38

S o, that's it, really. That's my story. Our story.

It's been over four years since I began writing it. Many things have changed. My grandfather has come to Israel to visit, and we have gone to Germany. When we met, I was surprised because he certainly didn't fit the stereotype of the Germans I'd seen in films. Though his hair is blond like Shoshanna's, he has dark eyes, like my mother, who is built exactly like him. They're both sort of chubby. But my grandfather has really long legs, exactly like mine. He's clever and funny. A little too sentimental for my taste, but I have to say that I like him. His life has been very different from ours. But we focus on our similarities and respect our differences and just enjoy being together.

I think I understand why Mimi couldn't tolerate another loss in her life, but I have been lucky enough to learn that when we refuse to acknowledge hurt and loss, it doesn't help us heal. It only makes us angry or depressed. And when we build walls around ourselves, we isolate ourselves from the people we love and who love us. I had done that. I'll probably do it again. But maybe the next time, I'll be able to stop myself before I hurt the people I love.

Sarah and I still hang out together. After the army, she and Matti got engaged. Yeah, that Matti. We still have our political differences, but we are both less adamant about who's right and who's wrong in the ongoing conflict between us and the Palestinians. She's also spent time with Maha. Once you have lunch with the "enemy," it's harder to make generalizations. None of us believe that the past should be forgotten, but maybe we can use it to build on rather than to destroy each other.

Ari never regretted going to prison rather than becoming part of the destruction. He still works with the refuseniks, but he's leaving for Spain next month to study guitar with a well-known teacher. He said he needed to leave Israel for a while, to live in a country where breathing was something you could take for granted. His first short story, about our Passover seder four years ago, was just published in a literary magazine.

And speaking of that Passover seder, Dahlia and Abed became close again, but they're still not married.

My sister has continued to play the violin and plays for her adorable baby girl, who is named Mimi. She's also studying to be a psychologist. And her husband, Gideon, who was my first major crush, plays with the Israeli Philharmonic. Much to both my pleasure and embarrassment, he forever brags about what a good catch his sister-in-law is.

Me? I served my two years in the Israeli army. I wasn't a hero like Ari. I sat behind a desk after my basic training, but I saw things and heard things that helped me decide what I want to do with my life. I believe that justice must be served. I want to be a lawyer so I can represent people who dare to think for themselves, people who don't buckle under just because someone in charge commands them to do something they think is unjust. I want to be an Israeli who stands up for people who are willing to stand up for themselves—Israelis or Palestinians. But you know me. I still have trouble keeping my mouth shut, so I'm sure I'll have plenty of battles to fight.

Maha and I continue to process the raw emotions that were exposed that Passover night. Sometimes we forget. We go to concerts together, shop, meet for lunch, walk arm and arm on the street. But other times our differences seem almost insurmountable. Sometimes we get angry and argue, but we've learned how to argue without destroying our relationship, which, I think, is very deep.

Her brother, Mohammad, was released from prison as part of an agreement. He became more militant there, and that's hard on her and on her family, but they also understand why he's so angry, even though I believe that his anger is somewhat unjustified. That, of course, was a bone of contention between us.

One day, not long ago, I stopped for a coffee on Ben Yehuda Street. I was studying for a test, and something made me look up. Maha and her brother were walking toward me. I recognized him from his pictures. He looked a lot older and a lot thinner, but he was very well-dressed. What I realized almost immediately was that Maha was going to pass by without saying anything to me.

"Maha," I called out.

I could see how uncomfortable she was, and I probably should have just said hello and left it at that. But we were way past that point in our relationship.

"I assume you're Mohammed, Maha's brother."

Mohammed merely nodded.

"Yes," Maha said, quickly. "This is Mohammed. We were just on our way—"

"Shut up," he said, under his breath.

"I beg your pardon," I said, as I stood up.

"Noa, please. Let it go," Maha pleaded.

Thirty-eight

"Why are you being so rude?" I asked him, ignoring Maha.

Without answering me, he stalked off. I stared at Maha, waiting for an explanation.

"He refuses to speak to Israelis since he got out of prison."

"But I'm your friend. I didn't do anything to him."

"But you're one of them."

"I'm also part of us. You and me."

"Noa, you have to understand what it was like for him. The conditions under which he had to live. The way he was humiliated every day by the Israeli soldiers guarding him."

"I wasn't one of those guards."

"But you are an Israeli."

"This is ridiculous. Haven't we gotten past that? Do you think it's okay for him to refuse to speak to me?"

"Yes, I do."

"Oh, Maha—"

"I think you might do the same thing if you were in his shoes."

"I hope not."

"How long did it take you to call me after Mimi was killed?" she asked, quietly.

We stood looking at each other for a moment; then I put my arms around her.

"Go—catch up with Mohammed. There's no reason for him to be angry with you, too."

She patted my back and ran down the street toward the lanky figure disappearing in the distance.

Maha is a medical student, just as she said she would be. If she got into legal trouble, I would defend her. And if I got sick, I believe she would heal me.

The conflict between Arabs and Jews goes back hundreds of years. Some people would say it goes back thousands of years to biblical times, back to the story of Abraham, who is the patriarch of both the Jews and the Muslims. All the Jewish tribes claim to be descended from Abraham and Sarah, while Arabs claim to be descended from Abraham and Hagar. And since biblical times the relationship between the descendents of the half-brothers, Isaac and Ishmael, has sometimes been peaceful and sometimes tumultuous, filled with jealousy and fear.

Can there ever be peace between the Palestinians and the Israelis? I don't know. Both sides have made major mistakes, and they continue to make them. I think we have to admit that, and so do they, before any real progress is made. Can the half-brothers learn to get along? Maybe. If Maha and I can present a united front, even when we disagree, then there's hope for all of us.

Milton Keynes UK
Ingram Content Group UK Ltd.
UKHW040740180824
446934UK00013B/146